CIRQUE DU FREAK

THE SAGA OF DARREN SHAN
BOOK 1

Other titles by
DARREN SHAN

THE SAGA OF DARREN SHAN

1 Cirque Du Freak*
2 The Vampire's Assistant*
3 Tunnels of Blood*
4 Vampire Mountain
5 Trials of Death
6 The Vampire Prince
7 Hunters of the Dusk
8 Allies of the Night
9 Killers of the Dawn
10 The Lake of Souls
11 Lord of the Shadows
12 Sons of Destiny

THE DEMONATA

1 Lord Loss*
2 Demon Thief*
3 Slawter*
4 Bec*
5 Blood Beast*
6 Demon Apocalypse*
7 Death's Shadow*
8 Wolf Island*

*Also available on audio

DARREN SHAN
CIRQUE DU FREAK

THE SAGA OF DARREN SHAN
BOOK 1

HarperCollins *Children's Books*

Madam Octa's on the web… and so is Darren Shan!
For all things freaky, check out the official
Darren Shan website at www.darrenshan.com

First published in Great Britain by HarperCollins *Children's Books* in 2000
This edition published 2009
HarperCollins *Children's Books* is a division of HarperCollins*Publishers* Ltd
77-85 Fulham Palace Road, Hammersmith
London W6 8JB

The HarperCollins website address is:
www.harpercollins.co.uk

1

Text copyright © 2000 Darren Shan

ISBN-13 978 0 00 794549 8

The author asserts the moral right to
be identified as the author of the work.

Printed and bound in Great Britain by
Clays Ltd, St Ives plc

This freakish show could never have gone public but for
the efforts of my hard-working laboratory assistants:

Biddy & Liam – 'The Gruesome Twosome'
'Diabolical' Domenica de Rosa
'Growling' Gillie Russell
Emma 'The Exterminator' Schlesinger
and
'Lord of the Crimson Night' – Christopher Little

Thanks are also due to my feasting companions:
the Horrible Creatures of HarperCollins. And the ghoulish
pupils of Askeaton Primary School (and others) who served as
willing guinea pigs and braved nightmares to make this book
as tight, dark and chilling as possible.

INTRODUCTION

I'VE ALWAYS been fascinated by spiders. I used to collect them when I was younger. I'd spend hours rooting through the dusty old shed at the bottom of our garden, hunting the cobwebs for lurking eight-legged predators. When I found one, I'd bring it in and let it loose in my bedroom.

It used to drive my mum mad!

Usually, the spider would slip away after no more than a day or two, never to be seen again, but sometimes they hung around longer. I had one who made a cobweb above my bed and stood sentry for almost a month. Going to sleep, I used to imagine the spider creeping down, crawling into my mouth, sliding down my throat and laying loads of eggs in my belly. The baby spiders would hatch after a while and eat me alive, from the inside out.

I loved being scared when I was little.

When I was nine, my mum and dad gave me a small tarantula. It wasn't poisonous or very big, but it was the greatest gift I'd ever received. I played with that spider almost every waking hour of the day. Gave it all sorts of treats: flies and cockroaches and tiny worms. Spoilt it rotten.

Then, one day, I did something stupid. I'd been watching

a cartoon in which one of the characters was sucked up by a vacuum cleaner. No harm came to him. He squeezed out of the bag, dusty and dirty and mad as hell. It was very funny.

So funny, I tried it myself. With the tarantula.

Needless to say, things didn't happen quite like they did in the cartoon. The spider was ripped to pieces. I cried a lot, but it was too late for tears. My pet was dead, it was my fault, and there was nothing I could do about it.

My parents nearly hollered the roof down when they found out what I'd done – the tarantula had cost quite a bit of money. They said I was an irresponsible fool, and from that day on they never again let me have a pet, not even an ordinary garden spider.

I started with that tale from the past for two reasons. One will become obvious as this book unfolds. The other reason is:

This is a true story.

I don't expect you to believe me – I wouldn't believe it myself if I hadn't lived it – but it is. Everything I describe in this book happened, just as I tell it.

The thing about real life is, when you do something stupid, it normally costs you. In books, the heroes can make as many mistakes as they like. It doesn't matter what they do, because everything comes good at the end. They'll beat the bad guys and put things right and everything ends up hunky-dory.

In real life, vacuum cleaners kill spiders. If you cross a busy road without looking, you get whacked by a car. If you fall out of a tree, you break some bones.

Real life's nasty. It's cruel. It doesn't care about heroes and happy endings and the way things should be. In real life, bad things happen. People die. Fights are lost. Evil often wins.

I just wanted to make that clear before I began.

One more thing: my name isn't really Darren Shan. Everything's true in this book, *except* for names. I've had to change them because... well, by the time you get to the end, you'll understand.

I haven't used *any* real names, not mine, my sister's, my friends or teachers. Nobody's. I'm not even going to tell you the name of my town or country. I daren't.

Anyway, that's enough of an introduction. If you're ready, let's begin. If this was a made-up story, it would begin at night, with a storm blowing and owls hooting and rattling noises under the bed. But this is a real story, so I have to begin where it really started.

It started in a toilet.

CHAPTER ONE

I WAS in the toilet at school, sitting down, humming a song. I had my trousers on. I'd come in near the end of English class, feeling sick. My teacher, Mr Dalton, is great about things like that. He's smart and knows when you're faking and when you're being serious. He took one look at me when I raised my hand and said I was ill, then nodded his head and told me to make for the toilet.

"Throw up whatever's bugging you, Darren," he said, "then get your behind back in here."

I wish every teacher was as understanding as Mr Dalton.

In the end, I didn't get sick, but still felt queasy, so I stayed on the toilet. I heard the bell ring for the end of class and everybody came rushing out on their lunch break. I wanted to join them but knew Mr Dalton would give out if he saw me in the yard so soon. He doesn't get mad if you trick him but he goes quiet and won't speak to you for ages, and that's almost worse than being shouted at.

So, there I was, humming, watching my watch, waiting. Then I heard someone calling my name.

"Darren! Hey, Darren! Have you fallen in or what?"

I grinned. It was Steve Leopard, my best friend. Steve's real surname was Leonard, but everyone called him Steve Leopard. And not just because the names sound alike. Steve used to be what my mum calls "a wild child". He raised hell wherever he went, got into fights, stole in shops. One day — he was still in a pushchair — he found a sharp stick and prodded passing women with it (no prizes for guessing where he stuck it!).

He was feared and despised everywhere he went. But not by me. I've been his best friend since Montessori, when we first met. My mum says I was drawn to his wildness, but I just thought he was a great guy to be with. He had a fierce temper, and threw scary tantrums when he lost it, but I simply ran away when that happened and came back again once he'd calmed down.

Steve's reputation had softened over the years — his mum took him to see a lot of good counsellors who taught him how to control himself — but he was still a minor legend in the schoolyard and not someone you messed with, even if you were bigger and older than him.

"Hey, Steve," I called back. "I'm in here." I hit the door so he'd know which one I was behind.

He hurried over and I opened the door. He smiled when he saw me sitting down with my trousers on. "Did you puke?" he asked.

"No," I said.

"Do you think you're gonna?"

"Maybe," I said. Then I leaned forward all of a sudden and made a sick noise. Bluurgh! But Steve Leopard knew me too well to be fooled.

"Give my boots a polish while you're down there," he said, and laughed when I pretended to spit on his shoes and rub them with a sheet of toilet paper.

"Did I miss anything in class?" I asked, sitting up.

"Nah," he said. "The usual crap."

"Did you do your history homework?" I asked.

"It doesn't have to be done until tomorrow, does it?" he asked, getting worried. Steve's always forgetting about homework.

"The day after tomorrow," I told him.

"Oh," he said, relaxing. "Even better. I thought... " He stopped and frowned. "Hold on," he said. "Today's Thursday. The day after tomorrow would be... "

"Got you!" I yelled, punching him on the shoulder.

"Ow!" he shouted. "That hurt." He rubbed his arm but I could tell he wasn't really hurt. "Are you coming out?" he asked then.

"I thought I'd stay in here and admire the view," I said, leaning back on the toilet seat.

"Quit messing," he said. "We were five-one down when I came in. We're probably six or seven down now. We need you." He was talking about football. We play a game every lunchtime. My team normally wins but we'd lost a lot of our best players. Dave Morgan broke his leg. Sam White transferred to another school when his family moved. And Danny Curtain had stopped playing football in order to spend lunch hanging out with Sheila Leigh, the girl he fancies. Idiot!

I'm our best full-forward. There are better defenders and midfielders, and Tommy Jones is the best goalkeeper in the whole school. But I'm the only one who can stand up front and score four or five times a day without fail.

"OK," I said, standing. "I'll save you. I've scored a hat trick every day this week. It would be a pity to stop now."

We passed the older guys — smoking around the sinks as usual — and hurried to my locker so I could change into my trainers. I used to have a great pair, which I won in a writing competition. But the laces snapped a few months ago and the rubber along the sides started to fall off. And then my feet grew! The pair I have now are OK but they're not the same.

We were eight-three down when I got on the pitch. It wasn't a real pitch, just a long stretch of yard with painted goal posts at either end. Whoever painted them was a right idiot. He put the crossbar too high at one end and too low at the other!

"Never fear, Hotshot Shan is here!" I shouted as I ran onto the pitch. A lot of players laughed or groaned, but I could see my team mates picking up and our opponents growing worried.

I made a great start and scored two goals inside a minute. It looked like we might come back to draw or win. But time ran out. If I'd arrived earlier we'd have been OK but the bell rang just as I was hitting my stride, so we lost nine-seven.

As we were leaving the pitch, Alan Morris ran into the yard, panting and red-faced. They're my three best friends: Steve Leopard, Tommy Jones and Alan Morris. We must be the oddest four people in the whole world, because only one of us – Steve – has a nickname.

"Look what I found!" Alan yelled, waving a soggy piece of paper around under our noses.

"What is it?" Tommy asked, trying to grab it.

"It's— " Alan began, but stopped when Mr Dalton shouted at us.

"You four! Inside!" he roared.

"We're coming, Mr Dalton!" Steve roared back. Steve is Mr Dalton's favourite and gets away with stuff that the rest of us couldn't do. Like when he uses swear words sometimes in his stories. If I put in some of the words Steve has, I'd have been kicked out long ago.

But Mr Dalton has a soft spot for Steve, because he's special. Sometimes he's brilliant in class and gets everything right, while other times he can't even spell his own name. Mr Dalton says he's a bit of an *idiot savant*, which mean he's a stupid genius!

Anyway, even though he's Mr Dalton's pet, not even Steve can get away with turning up late for class. So whatever Alan had, it would have to wait. We trudged back to class, sweaty and tired after the game, and began our next lesson.

Little did I know that Alan's mysterious piece of paper was to change my life forever. For the worse!

CHAPTER TWO

WE HAD Mr Dalton again after lunch, for history. We were studying World War II. I wasn't too keen on it, but Steve thought it was great. He loved anything to do with killing and war. He often said he wanted to be a mercenary soldier – one who fights for money – when he grew up. And he meant it!

We had maths after history, and – incredibly – Mr Dalton for a third time! Our usual maths teacher was off sick, so others had been filling in for him as best they could all day.

Steve was in seventh heaven. His favourite teacher, three classes in a row! It was the first time we'd had Mr Dalton for maths, so Steve started showing off, telling him where we were in the book, explaining some of the trickier problems as though speaking to a child. Mr Dalton didn't mind. He was used to Steve and knew exactly how to handle him.

Normally Mr Dalton runs a tight ship – his classes are fun but we always come out of them having learned something – but he wasn't very good at maths. He tried hard but we could tell he was in over his head, and while he was busy trying to come to grips with things – his head buried in the maths book, Steve by his side making "helpful" suggestions – the rest of us began to fidget and talk softly to each other and pass notes around.

I sent a note to Alan, asking to see the mysterious piece of paper he'd brought in. He refused at first to pass it around, but I kept sending notes and finally he gave in. Tommy sits just two seats over from him, so he got it first. He opened it up and began studying it. His face lit up while he was reading and his jaw slowly dropped. When he passed it on to me – having read it three times – I soon saw why.

It was a flyer, an advertising pamphlet for some sort of travelling circus. There was a picture of a wolf's head at the top. The wolf had its mouth open and saliva was dripping from its teeth. At the bottom were pictures of a spider and a snake, and they looked vicious too.

Just beneath the wolf, in big red capital letters, were the words:

CIRQUE DU FREAK

Underneath that, in smaller writing:

FOR ONE WEEK ONLY – CIRQUE DU FREAK!!
SEE:
SIVE AND SEERSA – THE TWISTING TWINS!
THE SNAKE-BOY! THE WOLF MAN! GERTHA TEETH!
LARTEN CREPSLEY AND HIS PERFORMING SPIDER – MADAM OCTA!
ALEXANDER RIBS! THE BEARDED LADY! HANS HANDS!
RHAMUS TWOBELLIES – WORLD'S FATTEST MAN!

Beneath all that was an address where you could buy tickets and find out where the show was playing. And right at the bottom, just above the pictures of the snake and spider:

NOT FOR THE FAINT-HEARTED!
CERTAIN RESERVATIONS APPLY!

"Cirque Du Freak?" I muttered softly to myself. Cirque was French for circus... Circus of Freaks! Was this a *freak show*?! It looked like it.

I began reading the flyer again, immersed in the drawings and descriptions of the performers. In fact, I was so immersed, I forgot about Mr Dalton. I only remembered him when I realised the room was silent. I looked up, and saw Steve standing alone at the head of the class. He stuck out his tongue at me and grinned. Feeling the hairs on the back of my neck prickle, I stared over my shoulder and there was Mr Dalton, standing behind me, reading the flyer, lips tight.

"What is this?" he snapped, snatching the paper from my hands.

"It's an advert, sir," I answered.

"Where'd you get it?" he asked. He looked really angry. I'd never seen him this worked up. "Where'd you get it?" he asked again.

I licked my lips nervously. I didn't know how to answer. I wasn't going to drop Alan in the soup – and I knew he wouldn't own up by himself: even Alan's best friends know he's not the bravest in the world – but my mind was stuck in low gear and I couldn't think of a reasonable lie. Luckily, Steve stepped in.

"Sir, it's mine," he said.

"Yours?" Mr Dalton blinked slowly.

"I found it near the bus stop, sir," Steve said. "Some old guy threw it away. I thought it looked interesting, so I picked it up. I was going to ask you about it later, at the end of class."

"Oh." Mr Dalton tried not to look flattered but I could tell he was. "That's different. Nothing wrong with an inquisitive mind. Sit down, Steve." Steve sat. Mr Dalton stuck a bit of Blu-Tack on the flyer and pinned it to the blackboard.

"Long ago," he said, tapping the flyer, "there used to be real freak shows. Greedy con men crammed malformed people in cages and— "

"Sir, what's *malformed* mean?" somebody asked.

"Someone who doesn't look ordinary," Mr Dalton said. "A person with three arms or two noses; somebody with no legs; somebody very short or very tall. The con men put these poor people – who were no different to you or me, except in looks – on display and called them freaks. They charged the public to stare at them, and invited them to laugh and tease. They treated the so-called "freaks" like animals. Paid them little, beat them, dressed them in rags, never allowed them to wash."

"That's cruel, sir," Delaina Price – a girl near the front – said.

"Yes," he agreed. "Freak shows were cruel, monstrous creations. That's why I got angry when I saw this." He tore down the flyer. "They were banned years ago, but every so often you'll hear a rumour that they're still going strong."

"Do you think the Cirque Du Freak is a real freak show?" I asked.

Mr Dalton studied the flyer again, then shook his head. "I doubt it," he said. "Probably just a cruel hoax. Still," he added, "if it *was* real, I hope nobody here would dream of going."

"Oh, no, sir," we all said quickly.

"Because freak shows were terrible," he said. "They pretended to be like proper circuses but they were cesspits of evil. Anybody who went to one would be just as bad as the people running it."

"You'd have to be really twisted to want to go to one of those, sir," Steve agreed. And then he looked at me, winked, and mouthed the words: "We're going!"

CHAPTER THREE

STEVE PERSUADED Mr Dalton to let him keep the flyer. He said he wanted it for his bedroom wall. Mr Dalton wasn't going to give it to him but then changed his mind. He cut off the address at the bottom before handing it over.

After school, the four of us — me, Steve, Alan Morris and Tommy Jones — gathered in the yard and studied the glossy flyer.

"It's got to be a fake," I said.

"Why?" Alan asked.

"They don't allow freak shows any more," I told him. "Wolf-men and snake-boys were outlawed years ago. Mr Dalton said so."

"It's not a fake!" Alan insisted.

"Where'd you get it?" Tommy asked.

"I stole it," Alan said softly. "It belongs to my big brother." Alan's big brother was Tony Morris, who used to be the school's biggest bully until he got thrown out. He's huge and mean and ugly.

"You *stole* from *Tony*?!?" I gasped. "Have you got a death wish?"

"He won't know it was me," Alan said. "He had it in a pair of trousers that Mum threw in the washing machine. I stuck a blank piece of paper in when I took this out. He'll think the ink got washed off."

"Smart," Steve nodded.

"Where did Tony get it?" I asked.

"There was a guy passing them out in an alley," Alan said. "One of the circus performers, a Mr Crepsley."

"The one with the spider?" Tommy asked.

"Yeah," Alan answered, "only he didn't have the spider with him. It was night and Tony was on his way back from the pub." Tony's not old enough to get served in a pub, but hangs around with older guys who buy drinks for him. "Mr Crepsley handed the paper to Tony and told him they're a travelling freak show who put on secret performances in towns and cities across the world. He said you had to have a flyer to buy tickets and they only give them to people they trust. You're not supposed to tell anyone else about the show. I only found out because Tony was in high spirits – the way he gets when he drinks – and couldn't keep his mouth shut."

"How much are the tickets?" Steve asked.

"Fifteen pounds each," Alan said.

"Fifteen pounds!" we all shouted.

"Nobody's going to pay fifteen pounds to see a bunch of freaks!" Steve snorted.

"I would," I said.

"Me too," Tommy agreed.

"And me," Alan added.

"Sure," Steve said, "but *we* don't have fifteen pounds to throw away. So it's academic, isn't it?"

"What does *academic* mean?" Alan asked.

"It means we can't afford the tickets, so it doesn't matter if we would buy them or not," Steve explained. "It's easy to say you *would* buy something if you know you *can't*."

21

"How much *do* we have?" Alan asked.

"Tuppence ha'penny," I laughed. It was something my dad often said.

"I'd love to go," Tommy said sadly. "It sounds great." He studied the picture again.

"Mr Dalton didn't think too much of it," Alan said.

"That's what I mean," Tommy said. "If Sir doesn't like it, it must be super. Anything that adults hate is normally brilliant."

"Are we sure we don't have enough?" I asked. "Maybe they have discounts for children."

"I don't think children are allowed in," Alan said, but he told me how much he had anyway. "Five pounds seventy."

"I've got twelve pounds exactly," Steve said.

"I have six pounds eighty-five pence," Tommy said.

"And I have eight pounds twenty-five," I told them. "That's more than thirty pounds in all," I said, adding it up in my head. "We get our pocket money tomorrow. If we pool our— "

"But the tickets are nearly sold out," Alan interrupted. "The first show was yesterday. It finishes Tuesday. If we go, it'll have to be tomorrow night or Saturday, because our parents won't let us out any other night. The guy who gave Tony the flyer said the tickets for both those nights were almost gone. We'd have to buy them tonight."

"Well, so much for that," I said, putting on a brave face.

"Maybe not," Steve said. "My mum keeps a wad of money in a jar at home. I could borrow some and put it back when we get our pocket money."

"You mean steal?" I asked.

"I mean *borrow*," he snapped. "It's only stealing if you don't put it back. What do you say?"

"How would we get the tickets?" Tommy asked. "It's a school night. We wouldn't be let out."

"I can sneak out," Steve said. "I'll buy them."

"But Mr Dalton snipped off the address," I reminded him. "How will you know where to go?"

"I memorised it," he grinned. "Now, are we gonna stand here all night making up excuses, or are we gonna go for it?"

We looked at each other, then — one by one — nodded silently.

"Right," Steve said. "We hurry home, grab our money, and meet back here. Tell your parents you forgot a book or something. We'll lump the money together and I'll add the rest from the pot at home."

"What if you can't steal — I mean, borrow the money?" I asked.

He shrugged. "Then the deal's off. But we won't know unless we try. Now: hurry!"

With that, he sprinted away. Moments later, making up our minds, Tommy, Alan and me ran too.

CHAPTER FOUR

THE FREAK show was all I could think about that night. I tried forgetting it but couldn't, not even when I was watching my favourite TV shows. It sounded so weird: a snake-boy, a Wolf Man, a performing spider. I was especially excited by the spider.

Mum and Dad didn't notice anything was up, but Annie did. Annie is my younger sister. She can be a bit annoying but most of the time she's cool. She doesn't run to Mum telling tales if I misbehave, and she knows how to keep a secret.

"What's wrong with you?" she asked after dinner. We were alone in the kitchen, washing up.

"Nothing's wrong," I said.

"Yes there is," she said. "You've been behaving funny all night."

I knew she'd keep asking until she got the truth, so I told her about the freak show.

"It sounds great," she agreed, "but there's no way you'd get in."

"Why not?" I asked.

"I bet they don't let children in. It sounds like a grown-up sort of show."

"They probably wouldn't let a brat like *you* in," I said nastily, "but me and the others would be OK." That upset her, so

I apologised. "I'm sorry," I said. "I didn't mean that. I'm just annoyed because you're probably right. Annie, I'd give anything to go!"

"I've got a make-up kit I could lend you," she said. "You can draw on wrinkles and stuff. It'd make you look older."

I smiled and gave her a big hug, which is something I don't do very often. "Thanks, sis," I said, "but it's OK. If we get in, we get in. If we don't, we don't."

We didn't say much after that. We finished drying and hurried into the TV room. Dad got back home a few minutes later. He works on building sites all over the place, so he's often late. He's grumpy sometimes but was in a good mood that night and swung Annie round in a circle.

"Anything exciting happen today?" he asked, after he'd said hello to Mum and given her a kiss.

"I scored another hat trick at lunch," I told him.

"Really?" he said. "That's great. Well done."

We turned the TV down while Dad was eating. He likes peace and quiet when he eats, and often asks us questions or tells us about his day at work.

Later, Mum went to her room to work on her stamp albums. She's a serious stamp collector. I used to collect too, when I was younger and more easily amused.

I popped up to see if she had any new stamps with exotic animals or spiders on them. She hadn't. While I was there, I sounded her out about freak shows.

"Mum," I said, "have you ever been to a freak show?"

"A what?" she asked, concentrating on the stamps.

"A freak show," I repeated. "With bearded ladies and wolf-men and snake-boys."

She looked up at me and blinked. "A snake-boy?" she asked. "What on Earth is a snake-boy?"

"It's a…" I stopped when I realised I didn't know. "Well, that doesn't matter," I said. "Have you ever been to one?"

She shook her head. "No. They're illegal."

"If they weren't," I said, "and one came to town, would you go?"

"No," she said, shivering. "Those sorts of things frighten me. Besides, I don't think it would be fair on the people in the show."

"What do you mean?" I asked.

"How would *you* like it," she said, "if you were stuck in a cage for people to look at?"

"I'm not a freak!" I said huffily.

"I know," she laughed, and kissed the top of my head. "You're my little angel."

"Mum, don't!" I grumbled, wiping my forehead with my hand.

"Silly," she smiled. "But imagine you had two heads or four arms, and somebody stuck you on show for people to make fun of. You wouldn't like that, would you?"

"No," I said, shuffling my feet.

"Anyway, what's all this about a freak show?" she asked. "Have you been staying up late, watching horror films?"

"No," I said.

"Because you know your Dad doesn't like you watching— "

"I wasn't staying up late, OK?" I shouted. It's really annoying when parents don't listen.

"OK, Mister Grumpy," she said. "No need to shout. If you don't like my company, go downstairs and help your father weed the garden."

I didn't want to go, but Mum was upset that I'd shouted at her, so I left and went down to the kitchen. Dad was coming in from the back and spotted me.

"So this is where you've been hiding," he chuckled. "Too busy to help the old man tonight?"

"I was on my way," I told him.

"Too late," he said, taking off his wellies. "I'm finished."

I watched him putting on his slippers. He has huge feet. He takes size 12 shoes! When I was younger, he used to stand me on his feet and walk me around. It was like being on two long skateboards.

"What are you doing now?" I asked.

"Writing," he said. My dad has pen pals all over the world, in America, Australia, Russia and China. He says he likes to keep in touch with his global neighbours, though I think it's just an excuse to go into his study for a nap!

Annie was playing with dolls and stuff. I asked if she wanted to come to my room for a game of bed-tennis using a sock for a ball, and shoes for rackets, but she was too busy arranging her dolls for a pretend picnic.

I went to my room and dragged down my comics. I have loads of cool comics, *Superman*, *Batman*, *Spiderman* and *Spawn*. *Spawn*'s my favourite. He's a superhero who used to be a demon in Hell. Some of the *Spawn* comics are quite scary but that's why I love them.

I spent the rest of the night reading comics and putting them in order. I used to swap with Tommy, who has a huge collection, but he kept spilling drinks on the covers and crumbs between the pages, so I stopped.

Most nights I go to bed by ten, but Mum and Dad forgot about me, and I stayed up until nearly half-past ten. Then Dad saw the light in my room and came up. He pretended to be cross but he wasn't really. Dad doesn't mind too much if I stay up late. Mum's the one who nags me about that.

"Bed," he said, "or I'll never be able to wake you in the morning."

"Just a minute, Dad," I told him, "while I put my comics away and brush my teeth."

"OK," he said, "but make it quick."

I stuck the comics into their box and stuffed it back up on the shelf over my bed.

I put on my pyjamas and went to brush my teeth. I took my time, brushed slowly, and it was almost eleven when I got into bed. I lay back, smiling. I felt very tired and knew I'd fall asleep in a couple of seconds. The last thing I thought about was the Cirque Du Freak. I wondered what a snake-boy looked like, and how long the bearded lady's beard was, and what Hans Hands and Gertha Teeth did. Most of all, I dreamed about the spider.

CHAPTER FIVE

THE NEXT morning, Tommy, Alan and me waited outside the gates for Steve, but there was no sign of him by the time the bell rang for class, so we had to go in.

"I bet he's dossing," Tommy said. "He couldn't get the tickets and now he doesn't want to face us."

"Steve's not like that," I said.

"I hope he brings the flyer back," Alan said. "Even if we can't go, I'd like to have the flyer. I'd stick it up over my bed and—"

"You couldn't stick it up, stupid!" Tommy laughed.

"Why not?" Alan asked.

"Because Tony would see it," I told him.

"Oh yeah," Alan said glumly.

I was miserable in class. We had geography first, and every time Mrs Quinn asked me a question, I got it wrong. Normally geography's my best subject, because I know so much about it from when I used to collect stamps.

"Had a late night, Darren?" she asked when I got my fifth question wrong.

"No, Mrs Quinn," I lied.

"I think you did," she smiled. "There are more bags under

29

your eyes than in the local supermarket!" Everybody laughed at that – Mrs Quinn didn't crack jokes very often – and I did too, even though I was the butt of the joke.

The morning dragged, the way it does when you feel let down or disappointed. I spent the time imagining the freak show. I made-believe I was one of the freaks, and the owner of the circus was a nasty guy who whipped everybody, even when they got stuff right. All the freaks hated him, but he was so big and mean, nobody said anything. Until one day, he whipped me once too often, and I turned into a wolf and bit his head off! Everybody cheered and I was made the new owner.

It was a pretty good daydream.

Then, a few minutes before break, the door opened and guess who walked in? Steve! His mother was behind him and she said something to Mrs Quinn, who nodded and smiled. Then Mrs Leonard left and Steve strolled over to his seat and sat down.

"Where were you?" I asked in a furious whisper.

"At the dentist's," he said. "I forgot to tell you I was going."

"What about— "

"That's enough, Darren," Mrs Quinn said. I shut up instantly.

At break, Tommy, Alan and me almost smothered Steve. We were shouting and pulling at him at the same time.

"Did you get the tickets?" I asked.

"Were you really at the dentist's?" Tommy wanted to know.

"Where's my flyer?" Alan asked.

"Patience, boys, patience," Steve said, pushing us away and laughing. "All good things to those who wait."

"Come on, Steve, don't mess us around," I told him. "Did you get them or not?"

"Yes and no," he said.

"What does *that* mean?" Tommy snorted.

"It means I have some good news, some bad news, and some

crazy news," he said. "Which do you want to hear first?"

"*Crazy* news?" I asked, puzzled.

Steve pulled us off to one side of the yard, checked to make sure no one was about, then began speaking in a whisper.

"I got the money," he said, "and sneaked out at seven o'clock, when Mum was on the phone. I hurried across town to the ticket booth, but do you know who was there when I arrived?"

"Who?" we asked.

"Mr Dalton!" he said. "He was there with a couple of policemen. They were dragging a small guy out of the booth – it was only a small shed, really – when suddenly there was this huge bang and a great cloud of smoke covered them all. When it cleared, the small guy had disappeared."

"What did Mr Dalton and the police do?" Alan asked.

"Examined the shed, looked around a bit, then left."

"They didn't see you?" Tommy asked.

"No," Steve said. "I was well hidden."

"So you didn't get the tickets," I said sadly.

"I didn't say that," he contradicted me.

"You *got* them?" I gasped.

"I turned to leave," he said, "and found the small guy behind me. He was tiny, and dressed in a long cloak which covered him from head to toe. He spotted the flyer in my hand, took it, and held out the tickets. I handed over the money and— "

"You got them!" we roared delightedly.

"Yes," he beamed. Then his face fell. "But there was a catch. I told you there was bad news, remember?"

"What is it?" I asked, thinking he'd lost them.

"He only sold me two," Steve said. "I had the money for four, but he wouldn't take it. He didn't say anything, just tapped the bit on the flyer about "certain reservations", then handed me a card which said the Cirque Du Freak only sold two tickets per flyer.

31

I offered him extra money – I had nearly seventy pounds in total – but he wouldn't accept it."

"He only sold you *two* tickets?" Tommy asked, dismayed.

"But that means … " Alan began.

"… only two of us can go," Steve finished. He looked around at us grimly. "Two of us will have to stay at home."

CHAPTER SIX

IT WAS Friday evening, the end of the school week, the start of the weekend, and everybody was laughing and running home as quick as they could, delighted to be free. *Except* a certain miserable foursome who hung around the schoolyard, looking like the end of the world had arrived. Their names? Steve Leonard, Tommy Jones, Alan Morris and me, Darren Shan.

"It's not fair," Alan moaned. "Who ever heard of a circus only letting you buy two tickets? It's stupid!"

We all agreed with him, but there was nothing we could do about it apart from stand around, stubbing the ground with our feet, looking sour.

Finally, Alan asked the question which was on everybody's mind.

"So, who gets the tickets?"

We looked at each other and shook our heads uncertainly.

"Well, Steve *has* to get one," I said. "He put in more money than the rest of us, and he went to buy them, so he has to get one, agreed?"

"Agreed," Tommy said.

"Agreed," Alan said. I think he would have argued about it,

except he knew he wouldn't win.

Steve smiled and took one of the tickets. "Who goes with me?" he asked.

"I brought in the flyer," Alan said quickly.

"Nuts to that!" I told him. "Steve should get to choose."

"Not on your life!" Tommy laughed. "You're his best friend. If we let him pick, he'll pick you. I say we fight for it. I have boxing gloves at home."

"No way!" Alan squeaked. He's small and never gets into fights.

"I don't want to fight either," I said. I'm no coward but I knew I wouldn't stand a chance against Tommy. His dad teaches him how to box properly and they have their own punching bag. He would have floored me in the first round.

"Let's pick straws for it," I said, but Tommy didn't want to. He has terrible luck and never wins anything like that.

We argued about it a bit more, until Steve came up with an idea. "I know what to do," he said, opening his school bag. He tore the two middle sheets of paper out of an exercise book and, using his ruler, carefully cut them into small pieces, each one roughly the same size as the ticket. Then he got his empty lunch box and dumped the paper inside.

"Here's how it works," he said, holding up the second ticket. "I put this in, put the top on and shake it about, OK?" We nodded. "You stand side by side and I'll throw the bits of paper over your heads. Whoever gets the ticket wins. Me and the winner will give the other two their money back when we can afford it. Is that fair enough, or does somebody have a better idea?"

"Sounds good to me," I said.

"I don't know," Alan grumbled. "I'm the youngest. I'm not able to jump as high as— "

"Quit yapping," Tommy said. "*I'm* the smallest, and I don't mind. Besides, the ticket might come out on the bottom of the pile, float down low and be in just the right place for the shortest person."

"All right," Alan said. "But no shoving."

"Agreed," I said. "No rough stuff."

"Agreed," Tommy nodded.

Steve put the top on the box and gave it a good long shake. "Get ready," he told us.

We stood back from Steve and lined up in a row. Tommy and Alan were side by side, but I kept out of the way so I'd have room to swing both arms.

"OK," Steve said. "I'll throw everything in the air on the count of three. All set?" We nodded. "One," Steve said, and I saw Alan wiping sweat from around his eyes. "Two," Steve said, and Tommy's fingers twitched. "Three!" Steve yelled, jerked off the lid and tossed the paper high up into the air.

A breeze came along and blew the bits of paper straight at us. Tommy and Alan started yelling and grabbing wildly. It was impossible to see the ticket in among the scraps of paper.

I was about to start grabbing, when all of a sudden I got an urge to do something strange. It sounded crazy, but I've always believed in following an urge or a hunch.

So what I did was, I shut my eyes, stuck out my hands like a blind man, and waited for something magical to happen.

As I'm sure you know, usually when you try something you've seen in a movie, it doesn't work. Like if you try doing a wheelie with your bike, or making your skateboard jump up in the air. But every once in a while, when you least expect it, something clicks.

For a second I felt paper blowing by my hands. I was going to grab at them but something told me it wasn't time. Then, a second later, a voice inside me yelled, "NOW!"

I shut my hands really fast.

The wind died down and the pieces of paper drifted to the

ground. I opened my eyes and saw Alan and Tommy down on their knees, searching for the ticket.

"It's not here!" Tommy said.

"I can't find it anywhere!" Alan shouted.

They stopped searching and looked up at me. I hadn't moved. I was standing still, my hands shut tight.

"What's in your hands, Darren?" Steve asked softly.

I stared at him, unable to answer. It was like I was in a dream, where I couldn't move or speak.

"He doesn't have it," Tommy said. "He can't have. He had his eyes shut."

"Maybe so," Steve said, "but there's *something* in those fists of his."

"Open them," Alan said, giving me a shove. "Let's see what you're hiding."

I looked at Alan, then Tommy, then Steve. And then, very slowly, I opened my right-hand fist.

There was nothing there.

My heart and stomach dropped. Alan smiled and Tommy started looking down at the ground again, trying to find the missing ticket.

"What about the other hand?" Steve asked.

I gazed down at my left-hand fist. I'd almost forgotten about that one! Slowly, even slower than first time, I opened it.

There was a piece of green paper smack-dab in the middle of my hand, but it was lying face down, and since there was nothing on its back, I had to turn it over, just to be sure. And there it was, in red and blue letters, the magical name:

CIRQUE DU FREAK.

I had it. The ticket was mine. I was going to the freak show with Steve. "YEEEEEEESSSSSSSSSSSSS!!!!" I screamed, and punched the air with my fist. I'd won!

CHAPTER SEVEN

THE TICKETS were for the Saturday show, which was just as well, since it gave me a chance to talk to my parents and ask if I could stay over at Steve's Saturday night.

I didn't tell them about the freak show, because I knew they would say no if they knew about it. I felt bad about not telling the whole truth, but at the same time, I hadn't really told a lie: all I'd done was keep my mouth shut.

Saturday couldn't go quickly enough for me. I tried keeping busy, because that's how you make time pass without noticing, but I kept thinking about the Cirque Du Freak and wishing it was time to go. I was quite grumpy, which was odd for me on a Saturday, and Mum was glad to see the back of me when it was time to go to Steve's.

Annie knew I was going to the freak show and asked me to bring her back something, a photo if possible, but I told her cameras weren't allowed (it said so on the ticket) and I didn't have enough money for a T-shirt. I told her I'd buy her a badge if they had them, or a poster, but she'd have to keep it hidden and not tell Mum and Dad where she'd got it if they found it.

Dad dropped me off at Steve's at six o'clock. He asked what

time I wanted to be collected in the morning. I told him midday if that was OK.

"Don't watch horror movies, OK?" he said before he left. "I don't want you coming home with nightmares."

"Oh, Dad!" I groaned. "Everyone in my class watches horror movies."

"Listen," he said, "I don't mind an old Vincent Price film, or one of the less scary Dracula movies, but none of these nasty new ones, OK?"

"OK," I promised.

"Good man," he said, and drove off.

I hurried up to the house and rang the bell four times, which was my secret signal to Steve. He must have been standing right inside, because he opened the door straightaway and dragged me in.

"About time," he growled, then pointed to the stairs. "See that hill?" he asked, speaking like a soldier in a war film.

"Yes, sir," I said, snapping my heels together.

"We have to take it by dawn."

"Are we using rifles or machine guns, sir?" I asked.

"Are you mad?" he barked. "We'd never be able to carry a machine gun through all that mud." He nodded at the carpet.

"Rifles it is, sir," I agreed.

"And if we're taken," he warned me, "save the last bullet for yourself."

We started up the stairs like a couple of soldiers, firing imaginary guns at imaginary foes. It was childish, but great fun. Steve 'lost' a leg on the way and I had to help him to the top. "You may have taken my leg," he shouted from the landing, "and you may take my life, but you'll never take my country!"

It was a stirring speech. At least, it stirred Mrs Leonard, who came through from the downstairs living room to see what the racket was. She smiled when she saw me and asked if I wanted anything to eat or drink. I didn't. Steve said he'd like some caviar and champagne, but it wasn't funny the way he said it, and I didn't laugh.

Steve doesn't get on with his mum. He lives alone with her — his dad left when Steve was very young — and they're always arguing and shouting. I don't know why. I've never asked him. There are certain things you don't discuss with your friends if you're boys. Girls can talk about stuff like that, but if you're a boy you have to talk about computers, football, war and so on. Parents aren't cool.

"How will we sneak out tonight?" I asked in a whisper as Steve's mum went back into the living room.

"It's OK," Steve said. "She's going out." He often called her *she* instead of *Mum*. "She'll think we're in bed when she gets back."

"What if she checks?"

Steve laughed nastily. "Enter my room without being asked? She wouldn't dare."

I didn't like Steve when he talked like that, but I said nothing in case he went into one of his moods. I didn't want to do anything that might spoil the show.

Steve dragged out some of his horror comics and we read them aloud. Steve has great comics, which are only meant for adults. My mum and dad would hit the roof if they knew about them!

Steve also has loads of old magazines and books about monsters and vampires and werewolves and ghosts.

"Does a stake have to be made out of wood?" I asked when I'd finished reading a Dracula comic.

"No," he said. "It can be metal or ivory, even plastic, as long as it's hard enough to go right through the heart."

"And that will kill a vampire?" I asked.

"Every time," he said.

I frowned. "But you told me you have to cut off their heads and stuff them with garlic and toss them in a river."

"Some books say you have to," he agreed. "But that's to make sure you kill the vampire's spirit as well as its body, so it can't come back as a ghost."

"Can a vampire come back as a ghost?" I asked, eyes wide.

"Probably not," Steve said. "But if you had the time, and wanted to make sure, cutting off the head and getting rid of it would be worth doing. You don't want to take any chances with vampires, do you?"

"No," I said, shivering. "What about werewolves? Do you need silver bullets to kill them?"

"I don't think so," Steve said. "I think normal bullets can do the job. You might have to use lots of them, but they should work."

Steve knows everything there is to know about horror facts. He's read every sort of horror book there is. He says every story has at least some bit of truth in it, even if most are made up.

"Do you think the Wolf Man at the Cirque Du Freak is a werewolf?" I asked.

Steve shook his head. "From what I've read," he said, "the wolf-men in freak shows are normally just very hairy guys. Some of them are more like animals than people, and eat live chickens and stuff, but they're not werewolves. A werewolf would be no good in a show, because it can only turn into a wolf when there's a full moon. Every other night, it would be a normal guy."

"Oh," I said. "What about the snake-boy? Do you— "

"Hey," he laughed, "save the questions for later. The shows long ago were terrible. The owners used to starve the freaks and keep them locked up in cages and treat them like dirt. But I don't know what this one will be like. They might not even be real freaks: they might only be people in costumes."

The freak show was being held at a place near the other side of town. We had to leave not long after nine o'clock, to make sure we got there in time. We could have got a cab, except we'd used most of our pocket money to replace the cash Steve took from his mum. Besides, it was more fun walking. It was spookier!

We told ghost stories as we walked. Steve did most of the talking, because he knows way more than me. He was on top form. Sometimes he forgets the ends of stories, or gets names mixed up, but not tonight. It was better than being with Stephen King!

It was a long walk, longer than we thought, and we almost didn't make it on time. We had to run the last half-kilometre. We were panting like dogs when we got there.

The venue was an old theatre which used to show movies. I'd passed it once or twice in the past. Steve told me once that it was shut down because a boy fell off the balcony and got killed. He said it was haunted. I asked my dad about it, and he said it was a load of lies. It's hard sometimes to know whether you should believe the stories your dad tells you or the ones your best friend tells you.

There was no name outside the door, and no cars parked nearby, and no queue. We stopped out front and bent over until we got our breath back. Then we stood and looked at the building. It was tall and dark and covered in jagged grey stones. Lots of the windows were broken, and the door looked like a giant's open mouth.

"Are you sure this is the place?" I asked, trying not to sound scared.

"This is what it says on the tickets," Steve said and checked again, just to be sure. "Yep, this is it."

"Maybe the police found out and the freaks had to move on," I said. "Maybe there isn't any show tonight."

"Maybe," Steve said.

I looked at him and licked my lips nervously. "What do you think we should do?" I asked.

He stared back at me and hesitated before replying. "I think we should go in," he finally said. "We've come this far. It'd be silly to turn back now, without knowing for sure."

"I agree," I said, nodding. Then I gazed up at the scary building and gulped. It looked like the sort of place you saw in a horror movie, where lots of people go in but don't come out. "Are you scared?" I asked Steve.

"No," he said, but I could hear his teeth chattering and knew he was lying. "Are *you*?" he asked.

"Course not," I said. We looked at each other and grinned. We knew we were both terrified, but at least we were together. It's not so bad being scared if you're not alone.

"Shall we enter?" Steve asked, trying to sound cheerful.

"Might as well," I said.

We took a deep breath, crossed our fingers, then started up the steps (there were nine stone steps leading up to the door, each one cracked and covered with moss) and went in.

CHAPTER EIGHT

WE FOUND ourselves standing in a long, dark, cold corridor. I had my jacket on, but shivered all the same. It was freezing!

"Why is it so cold?" I asked Steve. "It was warm outside."

"Old houses are like that," he told me.

We started to walk. There was a light down by the other end, so the further in we got, the brighter it became. I was glad of that. I don't think I could have made it otherwise: it would have been too scary!

The walls were scratched and scribbled-on, and bits of the ceiling were flaky. It was a creepy place. It would have been bad enough in the middle of the day, but this was ten o'clock, only two hours away from midnight!

"There's a door here," Steve said and stopped. He pushed it ajar and it creaked loudly. I almost turned and ran. It sounded like the lid of a coffin being tugged open!

Steve showed no fear and stuck his head in. He said nothing for a few seconds, while his eyes got used to the dark, then pulled back. "It's the stairs up to the balcony," he said.

"Where the kid fell from?" I asked.

"Yes."

"Do you think we should go up?" I asked.

He shook his head. "I don't think so. It's dark up there, no sign of any sort of light. We'll try it if we can't find another way in, but I think— "

"Can I help you boys?" somebody said behind us, and we nearly jumped out of our skins!

We turned around quickly and the tallest man in the world was standing there, glaring down on us as if we were a couple of rats. He was so tall, his head almost touched the ceiling. He had huge bony hands and eyes that were so dark, they looked like two black coals stuck in the middle of his face.

"Isn't it rather late for two little boys like yourselves to be out and about?" he asked. His voice was as deep and croaky as a frog's, but his lips hardly seemed to move. He would have made a great ventriloquist.

"We… " Steve began, but had to stop and lick his lips before he could continue. "We're here to see the Cirque Du Freak," he said.

"*Are* you?" The man nodded slowly. "Do you have tickets?"

"Yes," Steve said, and showed his.

"Very good," the man muttered. Then he turned to me and said: "How about you, Darren? Do you have a ticket?"

"Yes," I said, reaching into my pocket. Then I stopped dead in my tracks. *He knew my name!* I glanced at Steve and he was shaking in his boots.

The tall man smiled. He had black teeth and some were missing, and his tongue was a dirty shade of yellow. "My name is Mr Tall," he said. "I own the Cirque Du Freak."

"How did you know my friend's name?" Steve asked bravely.

Mr Tall laughed and bent down, so he was eyeball-to-eyeball with Steve. "I know lots of things," he said softly. "I know your names. I know where you live. I know you don't like your mummy or your daddy." He turned to face me and I took a step back. His breath stank to the high heavens. "I know you didn't tell your parents you were coming here. And I know how you won your ticket."

"*How?*" I asked. My teeth were shaking so much, I wasn't sure if he heard me or not. If he did, he decided not to answer, because next he stood up and turned away from us.

"We must hurry," he said, beginning to walk. I thought he would take giant steps, but he didn't, he took short ones. "The show is about to begin. Everyone else is present and seated. You are late, boys. You're lucky we didn't start without you."

He turned a corner at the end of the corridor. He was only two or three steps in front of us, but when we turned the corner, he was sitting behind a long table covered with a black cloth which reached down to the floor. He was wearing a tall red hat now, and a pair of gloves.

"Tickets, please," he said, reached out, took them, opened his mouth and put the tickets in, then chewed them to pieces and swallowed!

"Very well," he said. "You may go in now. We normally don't welcome children, but I can see you are two fine, courageous young men. We will make an exception."

There were two blue curtains in front of us, drawn across the end of the hall. Steve and me looked at each other and gulped.

"Do we walk straight on?" Steve asked.

"Of course," Mr Tall said.

"Isn't there a lady with a torch?" I asked.

He laughed. "If you want someone to hold your hand," he said, "you should have brought a baby-sitter!"

That made me mad and I forgot for a moment how afraid I was. "All right," I snapped, stepping forward, surprising Steve. "If that's the way it is... " I walked forward quickly and pushed past the curtains.

I don't know what those curtains were made of, but they felt like spider webs. I stopped once past. I was in a short corridor and another pair of curtains were draped across the walls a few metres in front. There was a sound behind and then Steve was by my side. We could hear noises on the other side of the curtains.

"Do you think it's safe?" I asked.

"I think it's safer to go forward than backwards," he answered. "I don't think Mr Tall would like it if we turned back."

"How do you think he knew all that stuff about us?" I asked.

"He must be able to read minds," Steve replied.

"Oh," I said, and thought about that for a few seconds. "He nearly scared the life out of me," I admitted.

"Me too," Steve said.

Then we stepped forward.

It was a huge room. The chairs had been ripped out of the theatre long ago, but deck chairs had been set up in their place. We looked for spare seats. The entire theatre was packed, but we were the only children there. I could feel people watching us and whispering.

The only spaces were in the fourth row from the front. We had to step over lots of legs to get there and people were grumbling. When we sat down, we realised they were good seats, because we were right in the middle and nobody tall was in front of us. We had a perfect view of the stage and could see everything.

"Do you think they sell popcorn?" I asked.

"At a freak show?" Steve snorted. "Get real! They might sell snake eggs and lizard eyes, but I'll bet anything you like they don't sell popcorn!"

The people in the theatre were a mixed bunch. Some were dressed stylishly, others in tracksuits. Some were as old as the hills, others just a few years older than Steve and me. Some chatted confidently to their companions and behaved as though at a football match, others sat quietly in their chairs and gazed around nervously.

What everyone shared was a look of excitement. I could see it in their eyes, the same light that was shining in Steve's and mine. We all somehow knew that we were in for something special, the like of which we'd never seen before.

Then a load of trumpets blew and the whole place went quiet. The trumpets blew for ages and ages, getting louder and louder, and every light went out until the theatre was pitch black. I began to get scared again, but it was too late to leave.

All of a sudden, the trumpets stopped and there was silence. My ears were ringing and for a few seconds I felt dizzy. Then I recovered and sat up straight in my seat.

Somewhere high up in the theatre, someone switched on a green light and the stage lit up. It looked eerie! For about a minute nothing else happened. Then two men came on, pulling a cage. It was on wheels and covered with what looked like a huge bearskin rug. When they got to the middle of the stage they stopped, dropped the ropes and ran back into the wings.

For a few seconds more – silence. Then the trumpets blew again, three short blasts. The rug came flying off the cage and the first freak was revealed.

That was when the screaming began.

CHAPTER NINE

THERE WAS no need for the screaming. The freak was quite shocking, but he was chained up inside the cage. I think the people who screamed did it for fun, the way people scream on a roller coaster, not because they were actually afraid.

It was the Wolf Man. He was very ugly, hair all over his body. He only wore a piece of cloth around his middle, like Tarzan, so we could see his hairy legs and belly and back and arms. He had a long bushy beard which covered most of his face. His eyes were yellow and his teeth were red.

He shook the bars of the cage and roared. It was pretty frightening. Lots more people screamed when he roared. I nearly screamed myself, except I didn't want to look like a baby.

The Wolf Man went on shaking the bars and jumping about, before calming down. When he was sitting on his backside, the way dogs do, Mr Tall walked on and spoke.

"Ladies and gentlemen," he said, and even though his voice was low and croaky, everybody could hear what he was saying, "welcome to the Cirque Du Freak, home of the world's most remarkable human beings.

"We are an ancient circus," he went on. "We have toured for

five hundred years, bringing the grotesque to generation after generation. Our line-up has changed many times, but never our aim, which is to astound and terrify you! We present acts both frightening and bizarre, acts you can find nowhere else in the world.

"Those who are easily scared should leave now," he warned. "I'm sure there are people who came tonight thinking this was a joke. Maybe they thought our freaks would be people in masks, or harmless misfits. *This is not so!* Every act you see tonight is real. Each performer is unique. And none are harmless."

That was the end of his speech and he walked offstage. Two pretty women in shiny suits came on next and unlocked the door of the Wolf Man's cage. A few people looked scared but nobody left.

The Wolf Man was yapping and howling when he first came out of the cage, until one of the ladies hypnotised him with her fingers. The other lady spoke to the crowd.

"You must be very quiet," she said in a foreign accent. "The Wolf Man will not be able to hurt you as long as we control him but a loud sound could wake him up, and then he would be deadly!"

When they were ready, they stepped down from the stage and walked the hypnotised Wolf Man through the theatre. His hair was a dirty grey colour and he walked with a stoop, fingers hanging down around his knees.

The ladies stayed by his side and warned people to be quiet. They let you stroke him if you wanted, but you had to do it gently. Steve rubbed him when he went by but I was afraid he might wake up and bite me, so I didn't.

"What did it feel like?" I asked, as quietly as I could.

"It was spiky," Steve replied, "like a hedgehog." He lifted his fingers to his nose and sniffed. "It smells strange too, like burning rubber."

The Wolf Man and ladies were about halfway down the rows of seats when there was a big BANG! I don't know what made the noise, but suddenly the Wolf Man began roaring and he shoved the ladies away from him.

People screamed and those nearest him leapt from their seats and ran. One woman wasn't quick enough, and the Wolf Man leapt on her and dragged her to the ground. She was screaming fit to burst, but nobody tried to help her. He rolled her over on to her back and bared his teeth. She stuck a hand up to push him away, but he got his teeth on it and *bit it off*!

A couple of people fainted when they saw that and loads more began yelling and running. Then, out of nowhere, Mr Tall appeared behind the Wolf Man and wrapped his arms around him. The Wolf Man struggled for a few seconds, but Mr Tall whispered something in his ear and he relaxed. While Mr Tall led him back to the stage, the women in the suits calmed down the crowd and told them to return to their seats.

While the crowd hesitated, the woman with the bitten-off hand went on screaming. Blood was pumping out of the end of her wrist, covering the ground and other people. Steve and me were staring at her, our mouths wide open, wondering if she was going to die.

Mr Tall returned from the stage, picked up the severed hand and gave a loud whistle. Two people in blue robes with hoods over their heads ran forward. They were short, not much bigger than me or Steve, but with thick arms and legs, and lots of muscles. Mr Tall sat the woman up and whispered something in her ear. She stopped screaming and sat still.

Mr Tall took hold of the wrist, then reached into his pocket and took out a small brown leather pouch. He opened it with his free hand and sprinkled a sparkly pink powder on to the bleeding wrist. Then he stuck the hand against it and nodded to the two people in the blue suits. They produced a pair of needles and loads of orange string. And then, to the amazement of everybody in the theatre, they started to stitch the hand back on to the wrist!

The people in blue robes stitched for five or six minutes. The woman didn't feel any pain, even though their needles were going in and out of her flesh, all the way around the wrist. When finished, they put their needles and unused thread away and returned to wherever they'd come from. Their hoods never slipped from their faces, so I couldn't tell if they were men or women. When they'd gone, Mr Tall let go of the woman's hand and stepped back.

"Move your fingers," he said. The woman stared at him blankly. "Move your fingers!" he said again, and this time she gave them a wiggle.

They moved!

Everybody gasped. The woman stared at the fingers as though she didn't believe they were real. She gave them another wiggle. Then she stood and lifted the hand above her head. She shook it as hard as she could, and it was good as new! You could see the stitches but there was no more blood and the fingers seemed to be working fine.

"You will be OK," Mr Tall told her. "The stitches will fall out after a couple of days. It will be fine after that."

"Maybe that's not good enough!" someone shouted, and a big red-faced man stepped forward. "I'm her husband," he said, "and I say we should go to a doctor and then the police! You can't let a wild animal like that out into a crowd! What if he'd bitten her head off?"

"Then she would be dead," Mr Tall said calmly.

"Listen, buster," the husband began, but Mr Tall interrupted.

"Tell me, sir," Mr Tall said, "where were *you* when the Wolf Man was attacking?"

"*Me?*" the man asked.

"Yes," Mr Tall said. "You are her husband. You were sitting beside her when the beast escaped. Why did you not leap to her rescue?"

"Well, I... There was no time... I couldn't... I wasn't... "

No matter what he said, the husband couldn't win, because there was only one true answer: he had been running away, looking after himself.

"Listen to me," Mr Tall said. "I gave fair warning. I said this show could be dangerous. This is not a nice, safe circus where nothing goes wrong. Mistakes can and do happen, and sometimes people end up a lot worse off than your wife. That's why this show is banned. That's why we must play in old theatres in the middle of the night. Most of the time, things go smoothly and nobody gets hurt. But we cannot guarantee your safety."

Mr Tall turned around in a circle and seemed to look everybody in the eye while turning. "We cannot guarantee *anybody's* safety," he roared. "Another accident like this is unlikely, but it *could* happen. Once again I say, if you are afraid, leave. Leave now, before it is too late!"

A few people did leave. But most stayed to see the rest of the show, even the woman who nearly lost her hand.

"Do you want to go?" I asked Steve, half-hoping he'd say yes. I was excited but scared as well.

"Are you crazy?" he said. "This is great! *You* don't want to go, do you?"

"No way," I lied, and slapped on a shaky little smile.

If only I hadn't been so scared of looking like a coward! I could have left and everything would have been fine. But no, I had to act like a big man and sit it out to the end. If you only knew how many times I've wished since then that I'd fled with all the speed in my body and never looked back...

CHAPTER TEN

As soon as Mr Tall had left the stage and we'd settled back into our seats, the second freak, Alexander Ribs, came on. He was more of a comedy act than a scary one, which was just what we needed to calm us down after the terrifying start. I happened to look over my shoulder while he was on, and noticed two of the blue-hooded people down on their knees, cleaning blood from the floor.

Alexander Ribs was the skinniest man I'd ever seen. He looked like a skeleton! There seemed to be no flesh on him. He would have been frightening, except he had a wide friendly smile.

Funny music played and he danced around the stage. He was dressed in ballet clothes and looked so ridiculous that soon everyone was laughing. After a while, he stopped dancing and began stretching. He said he was a contortionist (somebody with bones like rubber, who can bend every which-way).

First, he tilted his head back so far, it looked like it had been cut off. He turned round so we could see his upside-down face, then went on leaning backwards until his head was touching the floor! Then he put his hands round the backs of his legs and pulled his head through until it was sticking up in front of him.

It looked like it was growing out of his stomach!

He got a huge round of clapping for that, after which he straightened up and began twisting his body around like a curly-wurly straw! He kept twisting and twisting, five times around, until his bones began to creak from the strain. He stood like that for a minute, then began to unwind really, really fast.

Next, he got two drumsticks with furry ends. He took the first drumstick and hit one of his bony ribs with it. He opened his mouth and a musical note sprang out! It sounded like the noise pianos make. Then he closed his mouth and struck a rib on the other side of his body. This time it was a louder, higher note.

After a few more practice goes, he kept his mouth open and began playing songs! He played "London Bridge Is Falling Down", some songs by The Beatles, and the theme tunes from a few well-known TV shows.

The skinny man left the stage to shouts for more. But none of the freaks ever came back to do an encore.

After Alexander Ribs came Rhamus Twobellies, and he was as fat as Alexander was thin. He was eNORmous! The floorboards creaked as he walked out onto the stage.

He walked close to the edge and kept pretending he was about to topple forward. I could see people in the front rows getting worried, and some jumped back out of the way when he got close. I don't blame them: he would have squashed them flat as a pancake if he fell!

He stopped in the middle of the stage. "Hello," he said. He had a nice voice, low and squeaky. "My name is Rhamus Twobellies, and I really have two bellies! I was born with them, the same way certain animals are. The doctors were stunned and said I was a freak. That's why I joined this show and am here tonight."

The ladies who had hypnotised the Wolf Man came out with two trolleys full of food: cakes, chips, hamburgers, packets of sweets and heads of cabbage. There was stuff there that I hadn't even seen before, never mind tasted!

"Yum-yum," Rhamus said. He pointed to a huge clock being lowered by ropes from above. It stopped about three metres above his head. "How long do you think it will take me to eat all this?" he asked, pointing to the food. "There will be a prize for the person who guesses closest."

"An hour!" somebody yelled.

"Forty-five minutes!" somebody else roared.

"Two hours, ten minutes and thirty-three seconds," another person shouted. Soon everybody was calling out. I said an hour and three minutes. Steve said twenty-nine minutes. The lowest guess was seventeen minutes.

When we were finished guessing, the clock started to tick and Rhamus started to eat. He ate like the wind. His arms moved so fast, you could hardly see them. His mouth didn't seem to close at all. He shovelled food in, swallowed and moved on.

Everybody was amazed. I felt sick as I watched. Some people actually *were* sick!

Finally, Rhamus scoffed the last bun and the clock above his head stopped ticking.

Four minutes and fifty-six seconds! He'd eaten all that food in less than five minutes! I could hardly believe it. It didn't seem possible, even for a man with two bellies.

"That was nice," Rhamus said, "but I could have done with more dessert."

While we clapped and laughed, the ladies in shiny suits rolled the trolleys away and brought on a new one, packed with glass statues and forks and spoons and bits of metal junk.

"Before I begin," Rhamus said, "I must warn you not to try this at home! I can eat things which would choke and kill normal people. Do not try to copy me! If you do, you may die."

He began eating. He started with a couple of nuts and bolts, which he sucked down without blinking. After a few handfuls he gave his big round belly a shake and we could hear the noise of the metal inside.

His belly heaved and he spat the nuts and bolts back out! If there had only been one or two, I might have thought he was keeping them under his tongue or at the sides of his cheeks, but not even Rhamus Twobellies' mouth was big enough to hold that load!

Next, he ate the glass statues. He crunched the glass up into small pieces before swallowing it with a drink of water. Then he ate the spoons and forks. He twisted them up into circles with his hands, popped them into his mouth and let them slide down. He said his teeth weren't strong enough to tear through metal.

After that, he swallowed a long metal chain, then paused to catch his breath. His belly began rumbling and shaking. I didn't know what was going on, until he gave a heave and I saw the top of the chain come out of his mouth.

As the chain came out, I saw that the spoons and forks were wrapped around it! He had managed to poke the chain through the hoops inside his belly. It was unbelievable.

When Rhamus left the stage, I thought nobody could top such an act.

I was wrong!

CHAPTER ELEVEN

A COUPLE of people in the blue-hooded robes came around after Rhamus Twobellies, selling gifts. There was some really cool stuff, like chocolate models of the nuts and bolts that Rhamus ate, and rubber dolls of Alexander Ribs which you could bend and stretch. And there were clippings of the Wolf Man's hair. I bought a bit of that: it was tough and wiry, sharp as a knife.

"There will be more novelties later," Mr Tall announced from the stage, "so don't spend all your money right away."

"How much is the glass statue?" Steve asked. It was the same sort that Rhamus Twobellies had eaten. The person in the blue hood didn't say anything, but stuck out a sign with the price on. "I can't read," Steve said. "Will you tell me how much it costs?"

I stared at Steve and wondered why he was lying. The person in the hood still didn't speak. This time he (or she) shook his head quickly and moved on before Steve could ask anything else.

"What was that about?" I asked.

Steve shrugged. "I wanted to hear it speak," he said, "to see if it was human or not."

"Of course it's human," I said. "What else could it be?"

"I don't know," he said. "That's why I was asking. Don't you think it's strange that they keep their faces covered all the time?"

"Maybe they're shy," I said.

"Maybe," he said, but I could tell he didn't believe that.

When the people selling the gifts were finished, the next freak came on. It was the bearded lady, and at first I thought it was meant to be a joke, because she didn't have a beard!

Mr Tall stood behind her and said, "Ladies and gentlemen, this is a very special act. Truska here is new to our family. She is one of the most incredible performers I have ever seen, with a truly unique talent."

Mr Tall walked off. Truska was very beautiful, dressed in flowing red robes which had many slashes and gaps. Lots of the men in the theatre began to cough and shift around in their seats.

Truska stepped closer to the edge of the stage, so we could see her better, then said something that sounded like a seal barking. She put her hands on her face, one at either side, and stroked the skin gently. Then she held her nose shut with two fingers and tickled her chin with her other hand.

An extraordinary thing happened: she began to grow a beard! Hairs crept out, first on her chin, then her upper lip, then the sides of her face, finally all over. It was long and blonde and straight.

It grew about ten or eleven centimetres, then stopped. She took her fingers away from her nose and stepped down into the crowd, where she walked around and let people pull on the beard and stroke it.

The beard continued growing as she walked, until finally it reached down to her feet! When she arrived at the rear of the theatre, she turned and walked back to the stage. Even though there was no breeze in here, her hair blew about wildly, tickling people's faces as she passed.

When she was back on the stage, Mr Tall asked if anybody had a pair of scissors. Lots of women did. Mr Tall invited a few up.

"The Cirque Du Freak will give one solid bar of gold to anyone who can slice off Truska's beard," he said, and held up a small yellow ingot to show he wasn't joking.

That got a lot of people excited and for ten minutes nearly everybody in the theatre tried cutting off her beard. But they couldn't! Nothing could cut through the bearded lady's hair, not even a pair of garden shears which Mr Tall handed out. The funny thing was, it still felt soft, just like ordinary hair!

When everyone had admitted defeat, Mr Tall emptied the stage and Truska stood in the middle again. She stroked her cheeks as before and held her nose, but this time the beard grew back in! It took about two minutes for the hairs to disappear back inside, and then she looked exactly as she had when she first came out. She left to huge applause and the next act came on almost directly after.

His name was Hans Hands. He began by telling us about his father, who'd been born without legs. Hans' father learned to get around on his hands just as well as other people could on their feet, and had taught his children his secrets.

Hans then sat down, pulled up his legs and wrapped his feet around his neck. He stood on his hands, walked up and down the stage, then hopped off and challenged four men – picked at random – to a race. They could race on their feet; he'd race on his hands. He promised a bar of gold to anyone who could beat him.

They used the aisles of the theatre as a race track, and despite his disadvantage, Hans beat the four men easily. He claimed he could sprint a hundred metres in eight seconds on his hands, and nobody in the theatre doubted him. Afterwards he performed some impressive gymnastic feats, proving that a person could manage just as well without legs as with them. His act wasn't especially exciting but it was enjoyable.

There was a short pause after Hans had left, then Mr Tall came on. "Ladies and gentlemen," he said, "our next act is another unique and perplexing one. It can also be quite dangerous, so I ask that you make no noise and do not clap until you are told it is safe."

The whole place went quiet. After what had happened with the Wolf Man earlier, nobody needed telling twice!

When it was quiet enough, Mr Tall walked off the stage. He shouted out the name of the next freak as he went, but it was a soft shout: "Mr Crepsley and Madam Octa!"

The lights went down low and a creepy-looking man walked onto the stage. He was tall and thin, with very white skin and only a small crop of orange hair on the top of his head. He had a large scar running down his left cheek. It reached to his lips and made it look like his mouth was stretching up the side of his face.

He was dressed in dark-red clothes and carried a small wooden cage, which he put on a table. When he was set, he turned and faced us. He bowed and smiled. He looked even scarier when he smiled, like a crazy clown in a horror movie I once saw! Then he started to explain about the act.

I missed the first part of his speech because I wasn't looking at the stage. I was watching Steve. You see, when Mr Crepsley walked out, there had been total silence, except for one person who had gasped loudly.

Steve.

I stared curiously at my friend. He was almost as white as Mr Crepsley and was shaking all over. He'd even dropped the rubber model of Alexander Ribs that he'd bought.

His eyes were fixed on Mr Crepsley, as though glued to him, and as I watched him watch the freak, the thought which crossed my mind was: "He looks like he's seen a ghost!"

CHAPTER TWELVE

"IT IS not true that all tarantulas are poisonous," Mr Crepsley said. He had a deep voice. I managed to tear my eyes away from Steve and trained them on the stage. "Most are as harmless as the spiders you find anywhere in the world. And those which *are* poisonous normally only have enough poison in them to kill very small creatures.

"But some are deadly!" he went on. "Some can kill a man with one bite. They are rare, and only found in extremely remote areas, but they do exist.

"I have one such spider," he said and opened the door of the cage. For a few seconds nothing happened, but then the largest spider I had ever seen crawled out. It was green and purple and red, with long hairy legs and a big fat body. I wasn't afraid of spiders, but this one looked terrifying.

The spider walked forward slowly. Then its legs bent and it lowered its body, as though waiting for a fly.

"Madam Octa has been with me for several years," Mr Crepsley said. "She lives far longer than ordinary spiders. The monk who sold her to me said some of her kind live to be twenty or thirty years old. She is an incredible creature, both poisonous and intelligent."

hile he was speaking, one of the blue-hooded people led a goat onto the stage. It was making a frightened bleating noise and kept trying to run. The hooded person tied it to the table and left.

The spider began moving when it saw and heard the goat. It crept to the edge of the table, where it stopped, as if awaiting an order. Mr Crepsley produced a shiny tin whistle – he called it a flute – from his trouser pocket and blew a few short notes. Madam Octa immediately leaped through the air and landed on the goat's neck.

The goat gave a leap when the spider landed, and began bleating loudly. Madam Octa took no notice, hung on and moved a few centimetres closer to the head. When she was ready, she bared her fangs and sunk them deep into the goat's neck!

The goat froze and its eyes went wide. It stopped bleating and, a few seconds later, toppled over. I thought it was dead, but then realised it was still breathing.

"This flute is how I control Madam Octa," Mr Crepsley said, and I looked away from the fallen goat. He waved the flute slowly above his head. "Though we have been together such a long time, she is not a pet, and would surely kill me if I ever lost it.

"The goat is paralysed," he said. "I have trained Madam Octa not to kill outright with her first bite. The goat would die in the end, if we left it – there is no cure for Madam Octa's bite – but we shall finish it quickly." He blew on the flute and Madam Octa moved up the goat's neck until she was standing on its ear. She bared her fangs again and bit. The goat shivered, then went totally still.

It was dead.

Madam Octa dropped from the goat and crawled towards the front of the stage. The people in the front rows became very alarmed and some jumped to their feet. But they froze at a short command from Mr Crepsley.

"Do not move!" he hissed. "Remember your earlier warning: a sudden noise could mean death!"

Madam Octa stopped at the edge of the stage, then stood on her two back legs, the same as a dog! Mr Crepsley blew softly on his flute and she began walking backwards, still on two feet. When she reached the nearest leg of the table, she turned and climbed up.

"You will be safe now," Mr Crepsley said, and the people in the front rows sat down again, as slowly and quietly as they could. "But please," he added, "do not make any loud noises, because if you do, she might come after *me*."

I don't know if Mr Crepsley was really scared, or if it was part of the act, but he looked frightened. He wiped the sleeve of his right arm over his forehead, then placed the flute back in his mouth and whistled a strange little tune.

Madam Octa cocked her head, then appeared to nod. She crawled across the table until she was in front of Mr Crepsley. He lowered his right hand, and she crept up his arm. The thought of those long hairy legs creeping along his flesh made me sweat all over. And I *liked* spiders! People who were afraid of them must have been nervously chewing the insides of their cheeks to pieces.

When she got to the top of his arm, she scuttled along his shoulder, up his neck, over his ear, and didn't stop until she reached the top of his head, where she lowered her body. She looked like a funny sort of a hat.

After a while, Mr Crepsley began playing the flute again. Madam Octa slid down the other side of his face, along the scar, and walked around until she was standing upside-down on his chin. Then she spun a string of web and dropped down on it.

She was hanging about ten centimetres below his chin now, and slowly began rocking from side to side. Soon she was swinging about level with his ears. Her legs were tucked in, and from where I was sitting she looked like a ball of wool.

Then, as she made an upward swing, Mr Crepsley threw his head back and she went flying straight up into the air. The thread snapped and she tumbled around and around. I watched her go up, then come down. I thought she'd land on the floor or the table, but she didn't. Instead, she landed in Mr Crepsley's mouth!

I nearly got sick when I thought of Madam Octa sliding down his throat and into his belly. I was sure she'd bite him and kill him. But the spider was a lot smarter than I knew. As she was falling, she'd stuck her legs out and they had caught on his lips.

He brought his head forward, so we could see his face. His mouth was wide open and Madam Octa was hanging between his lips. Her body throbbed in and out of his mouth and she looked like a balloon which he was blowing up and letting the air out of.

I wondered where the flute was and how he was going to control the spider now. Then Mr Tall appeared with another flute. He couldn't play as well as Mr Crepsley, but he was good enough to make Madam Octa take notice. She listened, then moved from one side of Mr Crepsley's mouth to the other.

I didn't know what she was doing at first, so I craned my neck to see. When I saw the bits of white on Mr Crepsley's lips I understood: she was spinning a web!

When she was finished, she lowered herself from his chin, like she had before. There was a large web spun across Mr Crepsley's mouth. He began chewing and licking the web! He ate the whole of it, then rubbed his belly (being careful not to hit Madam Octa) and said, "Delicious. Nothing tastier than fresh spider webs. They are a treat where I come from."

He made Madam Octa push a ball across the table, then got her to balance on top of it. He set up small pieces of gym gear, tiny weights and ropes and rings, and put her through her paces.

She was able to do all the things a human could, like lift weights above her head and climb ropes and pull herself up on the rings.

Then he brought out a tiny dinner set. There were mini plates and knives and forks and teeny-weeny glasses. The plates were filled with dead flies and other small insects. I don't know what was in the glasses.

Madam Octa ate that dinner as neatly as you please. She was able to pick up the knives and forks, four at a time, and feed herself. There was even a fake saltcellar which she sprinkled over one of the dishes!

It was round about the time she was drinking from the glass that I decided Madam Octa was the world's most amazing pet. I would have given everything I owned for her. I knew it could never be — Mum and Dad wouldn't let me keep her even if I could buy her — but that didn't stop me from wishing.

When the act was over, Mr Crepsley put the spider back in her cage and bowed low while everybody clapped. I heard a lot of people saying it wasn't fair to have killed the poor goat, but it had been thrilling.

I turned to Steve to tell him how great I thought the spider was, but he was watching Mr Crepsley. He didn't look scared any more, but he didn't look normal either.

"Steve, what's wrong?" I asked.

He didn't answer.

"Steve?"

"Ssshhh!" he snapped, and wouldn't say another word until Mr Crepsley had left. He watched the odd-looking man walk back to the wings. Then he turned to me and gasped: "This is amazing!"

"The spider?" I asked. "It *was* great. How do you think—"

"I'm not talking about the spider!" he snapped. "Who cares about a silly old arachnid? I'm talking about Mr… Crepsley."

He paused before saying the man's name, as though he'd been about to call him something different.

"Mr Crepsley?" I asked, confused. "What was so great about him? All he did was play the flute."

"You don't understand," Steve said angrily. "You don't know who he really is."

"And *you* do?" I asked.

"Yes," he said, "as a matter of fact I do." He rubbed his chin and started looking worried again. "I just hope he doesn't know I know. If he does, we might never make it out of here alive..."

CHAPTER THIRTEEN

THERE WAS another break after Mr Crepsley and Madam Octa's act. I tried getting Steve to tell me more about who the man was, but his lips were sealed. All he said was: "I have to think about this." Then he closed his eyes, lowered his head and thought hard.

They were selling more cool stuff during the break: beards like the bearded lady's, models of Hans Hands and, best of all, rubber spiders which looked like Madam Octa. I bought two, one for me and one for Annie. They weren't as good as the real thing but they'd have to do.

They were also selling candy webs. I bought six of those, using up the last of my money, and ate two while waiting for the next freak to come out. They tasted like candy floss. I stuck the second one over my lips and licked at it, the same way Mr Crepsley had.

The lights went down and everybody settled back into their seats. Gertha Teeth was next up. She was a big woman with thick legs, thick arms, a thick neck and a thick head.

"Ladies and gentlemen, I am Gertha Teeth!" she said. She sounded strict. "I have the strongest teeth in the world! When I was a baby, my father put his fingers in my mouth, playing with me, and I bit two of them off!"

A few people laughed, but she stopped them with a furious look. "I am not a comedian!" she snapped. "If you laugh at me again, I will come down and bite your nose off!" That sounded quite funny, but nobody dared chuckle.

She spoke very loudly. Every sentence was a shout and ended in an exclamation mark (!).

"Dentists all over the world have been astounded by my teeth!" she said. "I have been examined in every major dental centre, but nobody has been able to work out why they are so tough! I have been offered huge amounts of money to become a guinea pig, but I like travelling and so I have refused!"

She picked up four steel bars, each about thirty centimetres long, but different widths. She asked for volunteers and four men went up on stage. She gave each of them a bar and said to try bending them. They did their best, but weren't able. When they had failed, she took the thinnest bar, put it in her mouth, and bit clean through it!

She handed the two halves back to one of the men. He stared at them in shock, then put one end in his own mouth and bit on it, to check that it was real steel. His howls when he almost cracked his teeth proved that it was.

Gertha did the same to the second and third bars, each of which was thicker than the first. When it came to the fourth, the thickest of the lot, she chewed it to pieces like a chocolate bar.

Next, two of the blue-hooded assistants brought out a large radiator and she bit holes in it! Then they gave her a bike and she gnashed it up into a little ball, tyres and all! I don't think there was anything in the world Gertha Teeth couldn't chew her way through if she set her mind to it.

She called more volunteers up on stage. She gave one a sledgehammer and a large chisel, one a hammer and smaller chisel, and the other an electric saw. She lay flat on her back and put the large chisel in her mouth. She nodded at the first volunteer to swing the sledgehammer at the chisel.

The man raised the sledgehammer high above his head and brought it down. I thought he was going to smash her face open and so did lots of others, judging by the gasps and people covering their hands with their eyes.

But Gertha was no fool. She swung out of the way and the sledgehammer slammed into the floor. She sat up and spat the chisel out of her mouth. "Hah!" she snorted. "How crazy do you think I am?"

One of the blue-hoods came out and took the sledgehammer from the man. "I only called you up to show the sledgehammer is real!" she told him. "Now," she said to those of us in the audience, "watch!"

She lay back again and stuck the chisel in her mouth. The blue-hood waited a moment, then raised the sledgehammer high and swung it down, faster and harder than the man had. It struck the top of the chisel and there was a fierce noise.

Gertha sat up. I expected to see teeth falling out of her mouth, but when she opened it and removed the chisel, there wasn't as much as a crack to be seen! She laughed and said: "Hah! You thought I had bitten off more than I could chew!"

She let the second volunteer go to work, the one with the smaller hammer and chisel. She warned him to be careful of her gums, then let him position the chisel on her teeth and whack away at them. He nearly hammered his arm off, but he wasn't able to harm them.

The third volunteer tried sawing them off with the electric saw. He ran the saw from one side of her mouth to the other, and sparks were flying everywhere, but when he put it down and the dust cleared, Gertha's teeth were as white, gleaming and solid as ever.

The Twisting twins, Sive and Seersa, came on after her. They were identical twins and they were contortionists like Alexander Ribs. Their act involved twisting their bodies around each other so they looked like one person with two fronts instead of a back, or two upper bodies and no legs. They were skilful and it was pretty interesting, but dull compared to the rest of the performers.

When Sive and Seersa were finished, Mr Tall came out and thanked us for coming. I thought the freaks would come out again and line up in a row, but they didn't. Instead, Mr Tall said we could buy more stuff at the back of the hall on our way out. He asked us to mention the show to our friends. Then he thanked us again for coming and said that the show was over.

I was a bit disappointed that it had ended so weakly, but it was late and I suppose the freaks were tired. I got to my feet, picked up the stuff I'd bought, and turned to say something to Steve.

He was looking behind me, up at the balcony, his eyes wide. I turned to see what he was looking at, and as I did, people behind us began to scream. When I looked up, I saw why.

There was a huge snake up on the balcony, one of the longest I had ever seen, and it was sliding down one of the poles towards the people at the bottom!

CHAPTER FOURTEEN

THE SNAKE'S tongue flicked in and out of its mouth and it seemed mighty hungry. It wasn't very colourful – dark green, with a few flecks of brighter colours here and there – but it looked deadly.

The people beneath the balcony ran back towards their seats. They were screaming and dropping stuff as they ran. A few people fainted and some fell and were crushed. Steve and me were lucky to be near the front: we were the smallest people in the theatre and would have been trampled to dust if we'd been caught in the rush.

The snake was about to slither onto the floor when a strong light fixed itself to the snake's face. The reptile froze and stared into the light without blinking. People stopped running and the panic died down. Those who had fallen pulled themselves back to their feet, and fortunately nobody appeared to be badly hurt.

There was a sound behind us. I turned to look back at the stage. A boy was up there. He was about fourteen or fifteen, very thin, with long yellowy-green hair. His eyes were oddly shaped, narrow like the snake's. He was dressed in a long white robe.

The boy made a hissing noise and raised his arms above his

head. The robe fell away and everybody who was watching him let out a loud gasp of surprise. His body was covered in scales!

From head to toe he sparkled, green and gold and yellow and blue. He was wearing a pair of shorts but nothing else. He turned around so we could see his back, and that was the same as the front, except a few shades darker.

When he faced us again, he lay down on his belly and slid off the stage, just like a snake. It was then that I remembered the snake-boy on the flyer and put two and two together.

He stood when he reached the floor and walked towards the back of the theatre. I saw, as he passed, that he had strange hands and feet: his fingers and toes were joined to each other by thin sheets of skin. He looked a bit like that monster I saw in an old horror film, the one who lived in the black lagoon.

He stopped a few metres away from the pillar and crouched down. The light which had been blinding the snake snapped off and it began to move again, sliding down the last stretch of pole. The boy made another hissing noise and the snake paused. I recalled reading somewhere once that snakes can't hear, but can feel sounds.

The snake-boy shuffled a short bit to his left, then his right. The snake's head followed him but didn't lunge. The boy crept closer to the snake, until he was within its range. I expected it to strike and kill him, and I wanted to scream at him to run.

But the snake-boy knew what he was doing. When he was close enough he reached out and tickled the snake beneath its chin with his odd webbed fingers. Then he bent forward and kissed it on the nose!

The snake wrapped itself around the boy's neck. It coiled about him a couple of times, leaving its tail draped over his shoulder and down his back like a scarf.

The boy stroked the snake and smiled. I thought he was going to walk through the crowd, letting the rest of us rub it, but he didn't. Instead he walked over to the side of the theatre, away from the path to the door. He unwrapped the snake and put it down on the floor, then tickled it under its chin once more.

The mouth opened wide this time, and I saw its fangs. The snake-boy lay down on his back a short bit away from the snake, then began wriggling towards it!

"No," I said softly to myself. "Surely he's not going to…"

But yes, he stuck his head in the snake's wide-open mouth!

The snake-boy stayed inside the mouth for a few more seconds, then slowly eased out. He wrapped the snake about him once more, then rolled around and around until the snake covered him completely, except for his face. He managed to hop to his feet and grin. He looked like a rolled-up carpet!

"And that, ladies and gentlemen," said Mr Tall from the stage behind us, "really is the end." He smiled and leapt from the stage, vanishing in midair in a puff of smoke. When it cleared, I saw him by the back of the theatre, holding the exit curtains open.

The pretty ladies and mysterious blue-hooded people were standing to his left and right, their arms loaded with trays full of goodies. I was sorry I hadn't saved some of my money.

Steve said nothing while we were waiting. I could tell from the serious look on his face that he was still thinking, and from past experience I knew there was no point trying to talk to him. When Steve went into one of his moods, nothing could jolt him out of it.

When the rows behind us had cleared out, we made our way to the back of the theatre. I brought the stuff I'd bought with me. I also lugged Steve's gifts, because he was so wrapped up in his thoughts, he would have dropped them or left them behind.

Mr Tall was standing at the back, holding the curtains open, smiling at everyone. The smile widened when we approached.

"Well, boys," he said, "did you enjoy the show?"

"It was fabulous!" I said.

"You weren't scared?" he asked.

"A little," I admitted, "but no more than anybody else."

He laughed. "You're a tough pair," he said.

There were people behind us, so we hurried on, not wanting to hold them up. Steve looked about when we entered the short corridor between the two sets of curtains, then leaned over and whispered in my ear: "Go back by yourself."

"What?" I asked, stopping. The people who had been behind us were chatting with Mr Tall, so there was no rush.

"You heard," he said.

"Why should I?" I asked.

"Because I'm not coming," he said. "I'm staying. I don't know how things will turn out, but I have to stay. I'll follow you home later, after I've... " His voice trailed off and he pulled me forward.

We pushed past the second set of curtains and entered the corridor with the table, the one covered by the long black cloth. The people ahead of us had their backs to us. Steve looked over his shoulder, to make sure nobody could see, then dived underneath the table and hid behind the cloth!

"Steve!" I hissed, worried he was going to get us into trouble.

"Go on!" he hissed back.

"But you can't— " I began.

"Do what I say!" he snapped. "Go, quick, before we're caught."

I didn't like it but what else could I do? Steve sounded like he'd go ape if I didn't obey him. I'd seen Steve get into fierce rages before and he wasn't someone you wanted to mess with when he was angry.

I started walking, turned the corner and began down the long corridor leading to the front door. I was walking slowly, thinking, and the people in front got further ahead. I glanced over my shoulder and saw there was still nobody behind me.

And then I spotted the door.

It was the one we'd stopped by on our way in, the one leading up to the balcony. I paused when I reached it and checked behind one last time. Nobody there.

"OK," I said to myself, "I'm staying! I don't know what Steve's up to, but he's my best friend. If he gets into trouble, I want to be there to help him out."

Before I could change my mind, I opened the door, slipped through, shut it quickly behind me and stood in the dark, my heart beating as fast as a mouse's.

I stood there for ages, listening while the last of the audience filed out. I could hear their murmurs as they discussed the show in hushed, frightened, but excited tones. Then they were gone and the place was quiet. I thought I'd be able to hear noises from inside the theatre, people cleaning up and fixing the chairs back in place, but the whole building was silent as a graveyard.

I climbed the stairs. My eyes had got used to the dark and I could see pretty well. The stairs were old and creaky and I was half-afraid they would snap under my feet and send me hurtling to my death, but they held.

When I reached the top I discovered I was standing in the middle of the balcony. It was very dusty and dirty up here, and cold too. I shivered as I crept down towards the front.

I had a great view of the stage. The lights were still on and I could see everything in perfect detail. Nobody was about, not the freaks, not the pretty ladies, not the blue-hoods — not Steve. I sat back and waited.

About five minutes later, I spotted a shadow creeping slowly towards the stage. It pulled itself up, then stood and walked to the centre, where it stopped and turned around.

It was Steve.

He started towards the left wing, then stopped and set off

towards the right. He stopped again. I could see him chewing on his nails, trying to decide which way to go.

Then a voice came from high above his head. "Are you looking for *me*?" it asked. A figure swooped down onto the stage, its arms out to its sides, a long red cloak floating behind it like a pair of wings.

Steve nearly jumped out of his skin when the figure hit the stage and rolled into a ball. I toppled backwards, terrified. When I rose to my knees again, the figure was standing and I was able to make out its red clothes, orange hair, pale skin and huge scar.

Mr Crepsley!

Steve tried speaking, but his teeth were shaking too much.

"I saw you watching me," Mr Crepsley said. "You gasped aloud when you first saw me. Why?"

"B-b-b-because I kn-kn-know who you a-are," Steve stuttered, finding his voice.

"I am Larten Crepsley," the creepy-looking man said.

"No," Steve replied. "I know who you *really* are."

"Oh?" Mr Crepsley smiled, but there was no humour in it. "Tell me, little boy," he sneered, "who am I, *really*?"

"Your real name is Vur Horston," Steve said, and Mr Crepsley's jaw dropped in astonishment. And then Steve said something else, and my jaw dropped too.

"*You're a vampire*," he said, and the silence which followed was as long as it was terrifying.

CHAPTER FIFTEEN

MR CREPSLEY (or Vur Horston, if that was his real name) smiled. "So," he said, "I have been discovered. I should not be surprised. It had to happen eventually. Tell me, boy, who sent you?"

"Nobody," Steve said.

Mr Crepsley frowned. "Come, boy," he growled, "do not play games. Who are you working for? Who put you onto me and what do they want?"

"I'm not working for anybody," Steve insisted. "I've lots of books and magazines at home about vampires and monsters. There was a picture of you in one of them."

"A *picture*?" Mr Crepsley asked suspiciously.

"A painting," Steve replied. "It was done in 1903, in Paris. You were with a rich woman. The story said the two of you almost married, but she found out you were a vampire and dumped you."

Mr Crepsley smiled. "As good a reason as any. Her friends thought she was inventing a fantastic story to make herself look better."

"But it wasn't a story, was it?" Steve asked.

"No," Mr Crepsley agreed. "It was not." He sighed and fixed Steve with a fierce gaze. "Though it might have been better for *you* if it had been!" he boomed.

If I'd been in Steve's place, I would have fled as soon as he said that. But Steve didn't even blink.

"You won't hurt me," he said.

"Why not?" Mr Crepsley asked.

"Because of my friend," Steve said. "I told him all about you and if anything happens to me, he'll tell the police."

"They will not believe him," Mr Crepsley snorted.

"Probably not," Steve agreed. "But if I turn up dead or go missing, they'll have to investigate. You wouldn't like that. Lots of police asking questions, coming here in the *daytime*... "

Mr Crepsley shook his head with disgust. "Children!" he snarled. "I hate children. What is it you want? Money? Jewels? The rights to publish my story?"

"I want to join you," Steve said.

I nearly fell off the balcony when I heard that. *Join him?*

"What do you mean?" Mr Crepsley asked, as stunned as I was.

"I want to become a vampire," Steve said. "I want you to make me a vampire and teach me your ways."

"You are crazy!" Mr Crepsley roared.

"No," Steve said, "I'm not."

"I cannot turn a child into a vampire," Mr Crepsley said. "I would be murdered by the Vampire Generals if I did."

"What are Vampire Generals?" Steve asked.

"Never you mind," Mr Crepsley said. "All you need to know is, it cannot be done. We do not blood children. It creates too many problems."

"So don't change me straightaway," Steve said. "That's OK. I don't mind waiting. I can be an apprentice. I know vampires often have assistants who are half-human, half-vampire. Let me be one. I'll work hard and prove myself, and when I'm old enough… "

Mr Crepsley stared at Steve and thought it over. He clicked his fingers while he was thinking and a chair flew up onto the stage from the front row! He sat down on it and crossed his legs.

"Why do you want to be a vampire?" he asked. "It is not much fun. We can only come out at night. Humans despise us. We have to sleep in dirty old places like this. We can never marry or have children or settle down. It is a horrible life."

"I don't care," Steve said stubbornly.

"Is it because you want to live forever?" Mr Crepsley asked. "If so, I must tell you – we do not. We live far longer than humans, but we die all the same, sooner or later."

"I don't care," Steve said again. "I want to come with you. I want to learn. I want to become a vampire."

"What about your friends?" Mr Crepsley asked. "You would not be able to see them again. You would have to leave school and home and never return. What about your parents? Would you not miss them?"

Steve shook his head miserably and looked down at the floor. "My dad doesn't live with us," he said softly. "I hardly ever see him. And my mum doesn't love me. She doesn't care what I do. She probably won't even notice I'm gone."

"That is why you want to run away? Because your mother does not love you?"

"Partly," Steve said.

"If you wait a few years, you will be old enough to leave by yourself," Mr Crepsley said.

"I don't want to wait," Steve replied.

"And your friends?" Mr Crepsley asked again. He looked quite kind at the moment, though still a bit scary. "Would you miss the boy you came with tonight?"

"Darren?" Steve asked, then nodded. "Yes, I'll miss my friends, Darren especially. But it doesn't matter. I want to be a vampire more than I care about them. And if you don't accept me, I'll tell the police and become a vampire hunter when I grow up!"

Mr Crepsley didn't laugh. Instead he nodded seriously. "You have thought this through?" he asked.

"Yes," Steve said.

"You are certain it is what you want?"

"Yes," came the answer.

Mr Crepsley took a deep breath. "Come here," he said. "I will have to test you first."

Steve stood beside Mr Crepsley. His body blocked my view of the vampire, so I couldn't see what happened next. All I know is, they spoke to each other very softly, then there was a noise like a cat lapping up milk.

I saw Steve's back shaking and I thought he was going to fall over but somehow he managed to stay upright. I can't even begin to tell you how frightened I was, watching this. I wanted to leap to my feet and cry out, "No, Steve, stop!"

But I was too scared to move, terrified that, if Mr Crepsley knew I was here, there would be nothing to stop him from killing and eating both me and Steve.

All of a sudden, the vampire began coughing. He pushed Steve away from him and stumbled to his feet. To my horror, I saw his mouth was red, covered in blood, which he quickly spat out.

"What's wrong?" Steve asked, rubbing his arm where he had fallen.

"You have bad blood!" Mr Crepsley screamed.

"What do you mean?" Steve asked. His voice was trembling.

"You are evil!" Mr Crepsley shouted. "I can taste the menace in your blood. You are savage."

"That's a lie!" Steve yelled. "You take that back!"

Steve ran at Mr Crepsley and tried to punch him, but the vampire knocked him to the floor with one hand. "It is no good," he growled. "Your blood is bad. You can never be a vampire!"

"Why not?" Steve asked. He had started to cry.

"Because vampires are not the evil monsters of lore," Mr Crepsley said. "We respect life. You have a killer's instincts, but we are not killers.

"I will not make you a vampire," Mr Crepsley insisted. "You must forget about it. Go home and get on with your life."

"No!" Steve screamed. "I won't forget!" He stumbled to his feet and pointed a shaking finger at the tall, ugly vampire. "I'll get you for this," he promised. "I don't care how long it takes. One day, Vur Horston, I'll track you down and kill you for rejecting me!"

Steve jumped from the stage and ran towards the exit. "One day!" he called back over his shoulder, and I could hear him laughing as he ran, a crazy kind of laugh.

Then he was gone and I was alone with the vampire.

Mr Crepsley sat where he was for a long time, his head between his hands, spitting bits of blood out onto the stage. He wiped his teeth with his fingers, then with a large handkerchief.

"Children!" he snorted aloud, then stood, still wiping his teeth, glanced one last time out over the chairs at the theatre (I ducked down low for fear he might spot me), then turned and walked back to the wings. I could see drops of blood dripping from his lips as he went.

I stayed where I was for a long, long time. It was tough. I'd never been as scared as I was up there on the balcony. I wanted to rush out of the theatre as fast as my feet would carry me.

But I stayed. I made myself wait until I was sure none of the freaks or helpers were about, then slowly crept back up the balcony, down the stairs, into the corridor, and finally out into the night.

I stood outside the theatre for a few seconds, staring up at the moon, studying the trees until I was sure there were no vampires lurking on any of the branches. Then, as quietly as I could, I raced for home. *My* home, not Steve's. I didn't want to be near Steve right then. I was almost as scared of Steve as I was of Mr Crepsley. I mean, he *wanted* to be a vampire! What sort of lunatic actually *wants* to be a vampire?

CHAPTER SIXTEEN

I DIDN'T ring Steve that Sunday. I told Mum and Dad we'd had a bit of an argument and that was why I'd come home early. They weren't happy about it, especially my having walked home so late at night by myself. Dad said he was going to dock my pocket money and was grounding me for a month. I didn't argue. The way I saw it, I was getting off lightly. Imagine what they'd have done to me if they knew about the Cirque Du Freak!

Annie loved her presents. She gobbled the candy down quick and played with the spider for hours. She made me tell her all about the show. She wanted to know what every freak looked like and what they'd done. Her eyes went wide when I told her about the Wolf Man and how he bit off a woman's arm.

"You're joking," she said. "That can't be true."

"It is," I vowed.

"Cross your heart?" she asked.

"Cross my heart."

"Swear on your eyes?"

"I swear on my eyes," I promised. "May rats gnaw them out if I'm telling a lie."

"Wow!" she gasped. "I wish I'd been there. If you ever go again, will you take me?"

"Sure," I said, "but I don't think the freak show comes here that often. They move about a lot."

I didn't tell Annie about Mr Crepsley being a vampire or Steve wanting to become one, but I thought about the two of them all day long. I wanted to ring Steve but didn't know what to say. He would be bound to ask why I didn't go back to his place, and I didn't want to tell him that I'd stayed in the theatre and spied on him.

Imagine: a real-life vampire! I used to believe they were real but then my parents and teachers convinced me they weren't. So much for the wisdom of grown-ups!

I wondered what vampires were really like, whether they could do everything the books and films said they could. I had seen Mr Crepsley make a chair fly, and I'd seen him swoop down from the roof of the theatre, and I'd seen him drink some of Steve's blood. What else could he do? Could he turn into a bat, into smoke, into a rat? Could you see him in a mirror? Would sunlight kill him?

As much as I thought about Mr Crepsley, I thought just as much about Madam Octa. I wished once again that I could buy one like her, one I could control. I could join a freak show if I had a spider like that, and travel the world, having marvellous adventures.

Sunday came and went. I watched TV, helped Dad in the garden and Mum in the kitchen (part of my punishment for coming home late by myself), went for a long walk in the afternoon, and daydreamed about vampires and spiders.

Then it was Monday and time for school. I was nervous going in, not sure what I was going to say to Steve, or what he might say to me. Also, I hadn't slept much over the weekend (it's hard to sleep when you've seen a real vampire), so I was tired and groggy.

Steve was in the yard when I arrived, which was unusual. I normally got to school before him. He was standing apart from the rest of the kids, waiting for me. I took a deep breath, then walked over and leaned against the wall beside him.

"Morning," I said.

"Morning," he replied. There were dark circles under his eyes and I bet he'd slept even less than me the last couple of nights. "Where did you get to after the show?" he asked.

"I went home," I told him.

"Why?" he asked, watching me carefully.

"It was dark outside and I wasn't looking where I was going. I took a few wrong turns and got lost. By the time I found myself somewhere familiar, I was closer to home than to your house."

I made the lie sound as convincing as possible, and I could see him trying to figure out if it was the truth or not.

"You must have got into a lot of trouble," he said.

"Tell me about it!" I groaned. "No pocket money, grounded for a month, and Dad said I'm going to have to do loads of chores. Still," I said with a grin, "it was worth it, right? I mean, was the Cirque Du Freak superb or what!"

Steve studied me for one more moment, then decided I was telling the truth. "Yeah," he said, returning my smile. "It was great."

Tommy and Alan arrived and we had to tell them everything. We were pretty good actors, Steve and me. You'd never have guessed that he had spoken to a vampire on Friday, or that I had seen him.

I could tell, as the day wore on, that things would never be quite the same between me and Steve. Even though he believed what I'd told him, part of him still doubted me. I caught him looking at me oddly from time to time, as though I was someone who had hurt him.

For my part, I didn't want to get too close to him any longer. It scared me, what he'd said to Mr Crepsley, and what the vampire had said to him. Steve was evil, according to Mr Crepsley. It worried me. After all, Steve was prepared to become a vampire and kill people for their blood. How could I go on being friends with someone like that?

We got chatting about Madam Octa later that afternoon. Steve and me hadn't said much about Mr Crepsley and his spider. We were afraid to talk about him, in case we let something slip. But Tommy and Alan kept pestering us and eventually we filled them in on the act.

"How do you think he controlled the spider?" Tommy asked.

"Maybe it was a fake spider," Alan said.

"It wasn't a fake," I snorted. "None of the freaks were fake. That was why it was so brilliant. You could tell everything was real."

"So how did he control it?" Tommy asked again.

"Maybe the flute is magic," I said, "or else Mr Crepsley knows how to charm spiders, the way Indians can charm snakes."

"But you said Mr Tall controlled the spider as well," Alan said, "when Mr Crepsley had Madam Octa in his mouth."

"Oh. Yes. I forgot," I said. "Well, I guess that means they must have used magic flutes."

"They didn't use magic flutes," Steve said. He had been quiet most of the day, saying less than me about the show, but Steve never could resist hammering someone with facts.

"So what *did* they use?" I asked.

"Telepathy," Steve answered.

"Is that something to do with telephones?" Alan asked.

Steve smiled, and Tommy and me laughed (although I wasn't entirely sure what "telepathy" meant, and I bet Tommy wasn't either). "Moron!" Tommy chuckled, and punched Alan playfully.

"Go on, Steve," I said, "tell him what it means."

"Telepathy is when you can read somebody else's mind," Steve explained, "or send them thoughts without speaking. That's how they controlled the spider, with their minds."

"So what's with the flutes?" I asked.

"Either they're just for show," Steve said, "or, more likely, you need them to attract her attention."

"You mean anyone could control her?" Tommy asked.

"Anyone with a brain, yes," Steve said. "Which counts you out, Alan," he added, but smiled to show he didn't mean it.

"You wouldn't need magic flutes or special training or anything?" Tommy asked.

"I wouldn't think so," Steve answered.

The talk moved on to something else after that — football, I think — but I wasn't listening. Because all of a sudden there was a new thought running through my mind, setting my brain on fire with ideas. I forgot about Steve and vampires and everything.

"You mean anyone could control her?"

"Anyone with a brain, yes."

"You wouldn't need magic flutes or special training or anything?"

"I wouldn't imagine so."

Tommy's and Steve's words kept bouncing through my mind, over and over, like a stuck CD.

Anyone could control her. That anyone could be *me*. If I could get my hands on Madam Octa and communicate with her, she could be my pet and I could control her and...

No. It was foolish. Maybe I could control her, but I would never own her. She was Mr Crepsley's and there was no way in the world that he would part with her, not for money or jewels or...

The answer hit me in a flash. A way to get her off him. A way to make her mine. *Blackmail!* If I threatened the vampire —

I could say I'd set the police onto him – he'd have to let me keep her.

But the thought of going face to face with Mr Crepsley terrified me. I knew I couldn't do it. That left just one other option: I'd have to *steal* her!

CHAPTER SEVENTEEN

EARLY MORNING would be the best time to steal the spider. Having performed so late into the night, most members of the Cirque Du Freak would probably sleep in until eight or nine. I'd sneak into camp, find Madam Octa, grab her and run. If that wasn't possible – if the camp was active – I'd simply return home and forget about it.

The difficult part was picking a day. Wednesday was ideal: the last show would have played the night before, so the circus would in all likelihood have pulled out before midday and moved on to its next venue before the vampire could awake and discover the theft. But what if they left town directly after the show, in the middle of the night? Then I'd miss my big chance.

It had to be tomorrow – Tuesday. That meant Mr Crepsley would have the whole of Tuesday night to search for his spider – for *me* – but that was a risk I'd just have to take.

I went to bed a bit earlier than usual. I was tired and ready to fall asleep, but was so excited, I thought I wouldn't be able to. I kissed Mum goodnight and shook Dad's hand. They thought I was trying to win my pocket money back, but it was in case something happened to me at the theatre and I never saw them again.

I have a radio which is also an alarm clock, and I set the alarm to five o'clock in the morning, then stuck my headphones on and plugged them into the radio. That way, I could wake up nice and early without waking anyone else.

I fell asleep quicker than I expected and slept straight through till morning. If I had any dreams, I can't remember them.

Next thing I knew, the alarm was sounding. I groaned, turned over, then sat up in bed, rubbing my eyes. I wasn't sure where I was for a few seconds, or why I was awake so early. Then I remembered the spider and the plan, and grinned happily.

The grin didn't last long, because I realised the alarm wasn't coming through my headphones. I must have rolled over in my sleep and pulled the cord out! I leapt across my bed and slammed the alarm off, then sat in the early morning darkness, heart pounding, listening for noises.

When I was sure my parents were still asleep, I slid out of bed and got dressed as quietly as I could. I went to the toilet and was about to flush when I thought of the noise it would make. I yanked my hand away from the lever and wiped the sweat from my brow. They would surely have heard that! A narrow escape. I'd have to be more careful when I got to the theatre.

I slipped downstairs and let myself out. The sun was on its way up and it looked like it would be a bright day.

I walked quickly and sang songs to pep me up. I was a bundle of nerves and almost turned back a dozen times. Once I actually *did* turn and start walking home, but then I remembered the way the spider had hung from Mr Crepsley's jaws, and the tricks she had performed, and swung around again.

I can't explain why Madam Octa meant so much to me, or why I was placing my life in such peril to have her. Looking back, I'm no longer sure what drove me on. It was simply a dreadful need I couldn't ignore.

The crumbling old building looked even creepier by day. I could see cracks running down the front, holes nibbled by rats and mice, spider webs in the windows. I shivered and hurried round to the rear. It was deserted. Empty old houses, junk yards, scrap heaps. There would be people moving about later in the day, but right then it looked like a ghost town. I didn't even see a cat or a dog.

As I'd thought, there were plenty of ways to get into the theatre. There were two doors and loads of windows to choose from.

Several cars and vans were parked outside the building. I didn't spot any signs or pictures on them, but I was sure they belonged to the Cirque Du Freak. It suddenly struck me that the freaks most probably slept in the vans. If Mr Crepsley had a home in one of them, my plan was sunk.

I snuck into the theatre, which felt even colder than it had been on Saturday night, and tiptoed down a long corridor, then another, then another! It was like a maze back here and I started worrying about finding my way out. Maybe I should go back and bring a ball of string, so I could mark my way and—

No! It was too late for that. If I left, I'd never have the guts to return. I'd just have to remember my steps as best I could and say a little prayer when it came time to leave.

I saw no sign of any freaks, and began to think I was on a fool's errand, that they were all in the vans or in nearby hotels. I'd been searching for twenty minutes and my legs felt heavy after so much walking. Maybe I should quit and forget the crazy plan.

I was about to give up when I found a set of stairs leading down to a cellar. I paused at the top for ages, biting my lips, wondering if I should go down. I'd seen enough horror films to know this was the most likely spot for a vampire, but I'd also seen loads where the hero walked down to a similar cellar, only to be attacked, murdered and chopped up into little pieces!

Finally I took a deep breath and started down. My shoes were making too much noise, so I eased them off and padded along in just my socks. I picked up loads of splinters, but was so nervous, I didn't feel the pain.

There was a huge cage near the bottom of the stairs. I edged over to it and looked through the bars. The Wolf Man was inside, lying on his back, asleep and snoring. He twitched and moaned as I watched. I jumped back from the cage. If he woke, his howls would bring the whole freak show down on me in seconds flat!

As I was stumbling backwards, my foot hit something soft and slimy. I turned my head slowly and saw I was standing over the snake-boy! He was stretched out on the floor, his snake wrapped around him, and his eyes were wide open!

I don't know how I managed not to scream or faint, but somehow I kept quiet and stayed on my feet, and that saved me. Because, even though the snake-boy's eyes were open, he was fast asleep. I knew by the way he was breathing: deeply, heavily, in and out.

I tried not to think about what would have happened if I'd fallen on him and the snake and woken them up.

Enough was enough. I gave one last look around the dark cellar, promising myself I'd leave if I didn't spot the vampire. For a few seconds I saw nothing and got ready to scram, but then I noticed what might have been a large box near one of the walls.

It *might* have been a large box. But it wasn't. I knew all too well what it really was. It was a coffin!

I gulped, then walked carefully over to the coffin. It was about two metres long and eighty centimetres wide. The wood was dark and stained. Moss was growing in patches, and I could see a family of cockroaches in one of the corners.

I'd love to say I was brave enough to lift the lid and peek inside, but of course I wasn't and didn't. Even the thought of *touching* the coffin gave me the shivers!

I searched for Madam Octa's cage. I felt sure she wouldn't be far from her master, and right enough, there was the cage, on the floor by the head of the coffin, covered by a big red cloth.

I glanced inside, to make sure, and there she was, her belly pulsing, her eight legs twitching. She looked horrible and terrifying this close up, and for a second I thought about leaving her. All of a sudden it seemed like a stupid idea, and the thought of touching her hairy legs or letting her anywhere near my face filled me with dread.

But only a true coward would turn back now. So I picked up the cage and laid it in the middle of the cellar. The key was hanging from the lock and one of the flutes was tied to the bars at the side.

I took out the note I had written back home the night before. It was simple, but had taken me ages to write. I read it as I stuck it to the top of the coffin with a piece of gum.

Mr Crepsley,
     I know who and what you are. I have taken Madam Octa and am keeping her. Do not come looking for her. Do not come back to this town. If you do, I will tell everyone that you are a vampire and you will be hunted down and killed. I am not Steve. Steve knows nothing about this. I will take good care of the spider.

Of course, I didn't sign it!

Mentioning Steve probably wasn't a good idea, but I was sure the vampire would think of him anyway, so it was just as well to clear his name.

With the note pinned in place, it was time to go. I picked up the cage and hurried up the stairs as fast as I could (being as silent as possible). I slipped my shoes back on and found my way out. It was easier than I'd imagined: the halls looked brighter after the dark of the cellar. When I got outside I walked slowly round to the front of the theatre, then ran for home, stopping for nothing, leaving the theatre and the vampire and my fear far behind. Leaving everything behind – except for Madam Octa!

CHAPTER EIGHTEEN

I MADE it back about twenty minutes before Mum and Dad got up. I hid the spider cage at the back of my wardrobe, under a pile of clothes, leaving enough holes so Madam Octa could breathe. She should be safe there: Mum left the tidying of the room to me, and hardly ever came in rooting around.

I slipped into bed and pretended to be asleep. Dad called me at a quarter to eight. I put on my school clothes and walked downstairs, yawning and stretching as though I'd only just woken. I ate breakfast quickly and hurried back upstairs to check on Madam Octa. She hadn't moved since I'd stolen her. I gave the cage a small shake but she didn't budge.

I would have liked to stay home and keep an eye on her but that was impossible. Mum always knows when I fake being sick. She's too smart to be fooled.

That day felt like a week. The seconds seemed to drag like hours, and even break and lunch-time went slowly! I tried playing football but my heart wasn't in it. I couldn't concentrate in class and kept giving stupid answers, even to simple questions.

Finally it ended and I was able to rush home and up to my room.

Madam Octa was in the same spot as earlier. I was half-afraid she was dead, but I could see her breathing. Then it struck me: she was waiting to be fed! I'd seen spiders this way before. They could sit still for hours at a time, waiting for their next meal to come along.

I wasn't sure what I should feed her, but I guessed it wasn't too different to what ordinary spiders ate. I hurried out into the garden, pausing only to snatch an empty jam jar from the kitchen.

It didn't take long to collect a couple of dead flies, a few bugs and a long wriggly worm, then back inside I raced, hiding the jam jar inside my T-shirt, so Mum couldn't see it and start asking questions.

I closed my bedroom door and stuck a chair against it so nobody could come in, then placed Madam Octa's cage on my bed and removed the cloth.

The spider squinted and crouched down lower at the sudden surge of light. I was about to open the door and throw the food in when I remembered I was dealing with a poisonous spider who could kill me with a couple of bites.

I lifted the jar over the cage, picked out one of the live insects and dropped it. It landed on its back. Its feet twitched in the air and then it managed to roll over onto its belly. It began crawling towards freedom but didn't get far.

As soon as it moved, Madam Octa pounced. One second she was standing still as a cocoon in the middle of the cage, the next she was over the insect, baring her fangs.

She swallowed the bug down quick. It would have fed a normal spider for a day or two, but to Madam Octa it was no more than a light snack. She made her way back to her original spot and looked at me as if to say, "OK, that was nice. Now where's the main course?"

I fed her the entire contents of the jar. The worm put up

a good fight, twisting and turning madly, but she got her fangs into it and ripped it in half, then into quarters. She seemed to enjoy the worm the most.

I had an idea and fetched my diary from underneath my mattress. My diary is my most prized possession, and it's because I wrote everything down in it that I'm able to write this book. I remember most of the story anyway, but whenever I get stuck, all I have to do is open the diary and check the facts.

I folded the diary open to the back page, then wrote down all that I knew about Madam Octa: what Mr Crepsley had said about her in the show, the tricks she knew, the food she liked. I put one tick beside food she liked a lot, and two ticks beside food she loved (so far, only the worm). This way I'd be able to work out the best way to feed her, and what to give her as a treat when I wanted her to do a trick.

I brought up some grub from the fridge next: cheese, ham, lettuce and corned beef. She ate just about everything I gave her. It looked like I was going to be kept busy trying to feed this ugly lady!

Tuesday night was horrible. I wondered what Mr Crepsley would think when he woke and found his spider missing and a note in its place. Would he leave like I told him, or would he come looking for his pet? Maybe, since the two of them could speak with each other telepathically, he would be able to trace her *here!*

I spent hours sitting up in bed, holding a cross to my chest. I wasn't sure if the cross would work or not. I know they work in the movies but I remembered talking to Steve once and he said a cross was no good by itself. He said they only worked if the person using them was good.

I finally fell asleep about two in the morning. If Mr Crepsley had come, I would have been completely defenceless, but luckily, when I woke in the morning, there was no sign of his having been, and Madam Octa was still resting in the wardrobe.

I felt a lot better that Wednesday, especially when I popped by the old theatre after school and saw the Cirque Du Freak had left. The cars and vans were gone. No trace of the freak show remained.

I'd done it! Madam Octa was mine!

I celebrated by buying a pizza. Ham and pepperoni. Mum and Dad wanted to know what the special occasion was. I said I just felt like something different, offered them — and Annie — a slice, and they left it at that.

I fed the scraps to Madam Octa and she loved them. She ran around the cage licking up every last crumb. I made a note in my diary: "For a special treat, a piece of pizza!"

I spent the next couple of days getting her used to her new home. I didn't let her out of the cage, but I carried it around the room so she could see every corner and get to know the place. I didn't want her to be nervous when I finally freed her.

I talked to her all the time, telling her about my life and family and home. I told her how much I admired her and the sort of food I was going to get her and the type of tricks we were going to do. She might not have understood everything I said, but she seemed to.

I went to the library after school on Thursday and Friday and read as much about spiders as I could find. There was all sorts of stuff I hadn't known. Like they can have up to eight eyes, and the threads of their webs are gluey fluids which harden when they're let out into the air. But none of the books mentioned performing spiders, or ones with telepathic powers. And I couldn't find any pictures of spiders like Madam Octa. It looked like none of the people who wrote these books had seen a spider like her. She was unique!

When Saturday came, I decided it was time to let her out of her cage and try a few tricks. I had practised with the flute and could play a few very simple tunes quite well. The hard part was sending thoughts to Madam Octa while playing. It was going to be tricky, but I felt I was up to it.

I closed my door and shut my windows. It was Saturday afternoon. Dad was working and Mum had gone to the shops with Annie. I was all alone, so if anything went wrong, it would be entirely my fault, and I would be the only one to suffer.

I placed the cage in the middle of the floor. I hadn't fed Madam Octa since last night. I figured she might not want to perform if she was full of food. Animals can be lazy, just like humans.

I removed the cloth, put the flute in my mouth, turned the key and opened the tiny door to the cage. I stepped back and squatted down low, so she could see me.

Madam Octa did nothing for a while. Then she crept to the door, paused and sniffed the air. She looked too fat to squeeze through the gap, and I began to think I must have overfed her. But somehow she managed to suck her sides in and ease out.

She sat on the carpet in front of the cage, her big round belly throbbing. I thought she might walk around the cage, to check the room out, but she didn't show the faintest sign of having any interest in the room.

Her eyes were glued to *me!*

I gulped loudly and tried not to let her sense my fear. It was difficult but I managed not to shake or cry. The flute had slipped a couple of centimetres from my lips while I was watching her but I was still holding it. It was time to start playing, so I pressed it back between my lips and prepared to blow.

That was when she made her move. In one giant leap, she sprang across the room. She flew forward, up into the air, jaws open, fangs ready, hairy legs twitching — *straight at my unprotected face!*

CHAPTER NINETEEN

IF SHE had connected, she would have sunk her fangs into me and I would have died. But luck was on my side, and instead of landing on flesh, she slammed against the end of the flute and went flying off to the side.

She landed in a ball and was dazed for a couple of seconds. Reacting rapidly, aware that my life depended on speed, I stuck the flute between my lips and played like a madman. My mouth was dry but I blew regardless, not daring to lick my lips.

Madam Octa cocked her head when she heard the music. She struggled to her legs and swayed from side to side, as though drunk. I sneaked a quick breath, then started playing a slower tune, which wouldn't tire my fingers or lungs.

"Hello, Madam Octa," I said inside my head, shutting my eyes and concentrating. "My name's Darren Shan. I've told you that before but I don't know if you heard. I'm not even sure if you can hear it now.

"I'm your new owner. I'm going to treat you real good and feed you loads of insects and meat. But only if *you* are good and do everything I tell you and don't attack me again."

She had stopped swaying and was staring at me. I wasn't sure if she was listening to my thoughts or planning her next leap.

"I want you to stand on your back legs now," I told her. "I want you to stand on your two back legs and take a little bow."

For a few seconds she didn't respond. I went on playing and thinking, asking her to stand, then commanding her, then begging her. Finally, when I was almost out of breath, she raised herself and stood on her two legs, the way I wanted. Then she took a little bow and relaxed, awaiting my next order.

She was obeying me!

The next order I gave was for her to crawl back into her cage. She did as I bid, and this time I only had to think it once. As soon as she was inside, I closed the door and fell back on my bum, letting the flute fall from my mouth.

The shock I'd got when she jumped at me! My heart was beating so fast, I was afraid it was going to run up my neck and leap out of my mouth! I lay on the floor for ages, staring at the spider, thinking about how close to death I had come.

That should have been warning enough. Any sensible person would have left the door shut and forgot about playing with such a deadly pet. It was too dangerous. What if she hadn't hit the flute? What if Mum had come home and found me dead on the floor? What if the spider then attacked her or Dad or Annie? Only the world's dumbest person would run a risk like that again.

Step forward – Darren Shan!

It was crazy, but I couldn't stop myself. Besides, the way I saw it, there was no point having stolen her if I was going to keep her locked up in a silly old cage.

I was a bit cleverer this time. I unlocked the door but didn't open it. Instead I played the flute and told *her* to push it open. She did, and when she came out she seemed as harmless as a kitten and did everything I'd communicated.

I made her do lots of tricks. Made her hop about the room

like a kangaroo. Then had her hang from the ceiling and draw pictures with her webs. Next I got her lifting weights (a pen, a box of matches, a marble). After that I told her to sit in one of my remote control cars. I turned it on and it looked like she was driving! I crashed it into a pile of books, but made her jump off at the last moment, so she wasn't hurt.

I played with her for about an hour and would have happily continued all afternoon, but I heard Mum arriving home and knew she would think it odd if I stayed up in my room all day. The last thing I wanted was her or Dad prying into my private affairs.

So I stuck Madam Octa back in the wardrobe and trotted downstairs, trying to look as natural as possible.

"Were you playing a CD up there?" Mum asked. She had four bags full of clothes and hats, which she and Annie were unpacking on the kitchen table.

"No," I said.

"I thought I heard music," she said.

"I was playing a flute," I told her, trying to sound casual.

She stopped unpacking. "*You?*" she asked. "Playing a *flute?*"

"I do know how to play one," I said. "You taught me when I was five years old, remember?"

"I remember," she laughed. "I also remember when you were six and told me flutes were for girls. You swore you were never going to look at one again!"

I shrugged as though it was no big thing. "I changed my mind," I said. "I found a flute on the way home from school yesterday and got to wondering if I could still play."

"Where did you find it?" she asked.

"On the road."

"I hope you washed it out before you put it in your mouth. There's no telling where it might have been."

"I washed it," I lied.

"This is a lovely surprise," she smiled, then ruffled my hair and gave my cheek a big wet kiss.

"Hey! Quit it!" I yelled.

"We'll make a Mozart out of you yet," she said. "I can see it now: you playing a piano in a huge concert hall, dressed in a beautiful white suit, your father and I in the front row..."

"Get real, Mum," I chuckled. "It's only a flute."

"From small acorns, oak trees grow," she said.

"He's as thick as an oak tree," Annie giggled.

I stuck my tongue out at her in response.

The next few days were great. I played with Madam Octa whenever I could, feeding her every afternoon (she only needed one meal a day, as long as it was a large one). And I didn't have to worry about locking my bedroom door because Mum and Dad agreed not to enter when they heard me practising the flute.

I considered telling Annie about Madam Octa but decided to wait a while longer. I was getting on well with the spider but could tell she was still uneasy around me. I wouldn't bring Annie in until I was sure it was completely safe.

My schoolwork improved during the next week, and so did my goal-scoring. I scored twenty-eight goals between Monday and Friday. Even Mr Dalton was impressed.

"With your good marks in class and your prowess on the field," he said, "you could turn into the world's first professional footballer-cum-university professor! A cross between Pele and Einstein!"

I knew he was only pulling my leg but it was nice of him to say it all the same.

It took ages to work up the nerve to let Madam Octa climb up my body and over my face, but I finally tried it on Friday afternoon. I played my best song and didn't let her start until I'd told her several times what I wanted her to do. When I thought we were ready, I gave her the nod and she began creeping up the leg of my trousers.

It was fine until she reached my neck. The feel of those long thin hairy legs almost caused me to drop the flute. I would have been a dead duck if I had, because she was in the perfect place to sink her fangs. Luckily, my nerve held and I went on playing.

She crawled over my left ear and up to the top of my head, where she lay down for a rest. My scalp itched beneath her but I had sense enough not to try scratching it. I studied myself in the mirror and grinned. She looked like one of those French hats, a beret.

I made her slide down my face and dangle from my nose on one of her web-strings. I didn't let her into my mouth, but I got her to swing from side to side like she'd done with Mr Crepsley, and had her tickle my chin with her legs.

I didn't let her tickle me too much, in case I started laughing and dropped the flute!

When I put her back in her cage that Friday night, I felt like a king, like nothing could ever go wrong, that my whole life was going to be perfect. I was doing well in school and at football, and had the sort of pet any boy would trade all his worldly goods for. I couldn't have been happier if I'd won the lottery or a chocolate factory.

That, of course, was when everything went wrong and the whole world crashed down around my ears.

CHAPTER TWENTY

STEVE POPPED over for a visit late Saturday afternoon. We hadn't said much to each other all week and he was the last person I was expecting. Mum let him in and called me downstairs. I saw him when I was halfway down, paused, then shouted for him to come up.

He gazed about my room as though he hadn't been here for months. "I'd almost forgotten what this place looks like," he said.

"Don't be silly," I said. "You were here a couple of weeks ago."

"It seems longer." He sat on the bed and turned his eyes on me. His face was serious and lonely. "Why have you been avoiding me?" he asked softly.

"What do you mean?" I pretended I didn't know what he was talking about.

"You've been steering clear of me these past two weeks," he said. "It wasn't obvious at first, but each day you've been spending less time with me. You didn't even pick me when we were playing basketball in P.E. last Thursday."

"You're not very good at basketball," I said. It was a lame excuse, but I couldn't think of a better one.

"I was confused at first," Steve said, "but then I figured it out. You didn't get lost the night of the freak show, did you? You stuck around, up in the balcony probably, and saw what happened between me and Vur Horston."

"I saw nothing of the sort," I snapped.

"No?" he asked.

"No," I lied.

"You didn't see anything?"

"No."

"You didn't see me talking to Vur Horston?"

"No!"

"You didn't— "

"Look, Steve," I interrupted, "whatever happened between you and Mr Crepsley is your business. I wasn't there, didn't see it, don't know what you're talking about. Now if— "

"Don't lie to me, Darren," he said.

"I'm not lying!" I lied.

"Then how did you know I was talking about Mr Crepsley?" he asked.

"Because. . . " I bit my tongue.

"I said I was talking to *Vur Horston*," Steve smiled. "Unless you were there, how would you know that Vur Horston and Larten Crepsley are one and the same?"

My shoulders sagged. I sat on the bed beside Steve. "OK," I said, "I admit it. I was in the balcony."

"How much did you see and hear?" Steve asked.

"Everything. I couldn't see what he was doing when he was sucking out your blood, or hear what he was saying. But apart from that. . . "

". . .everything," Steve finished with a sigh. "That's why you've been avoiding me: because he said I was evil."

"Partly," I said. "But mostly because of what *you* said. Steve, you asked him to turn you into a vampire! What if he *had* turned you into one and you'd come after me? Most vampires go after people they know first, don't they?"

"In books and films, yes," Steve said. "This is different. This is real life. I wouldn't have hurt you, Darren."

"Maybe," I said. "Maybe not. The point is, I don't want to find out. I don't want to be friends with you any more. You could be dangerous. What if you met another vampire and this one granted your wish? Or what if Mr Crepsley was right and you're really evil and— "

"I'm not evil!" Steve shouted, and shoved me back on the bed. He leapt on my chest and stuck his fingers in my face. "Take that back!" he roared. "Take that back, or so help me, I'll jerk your head off and— "

"I take it back! I take it back!" I shrieked. Steve was heavy on my chest, his face flushed and furious. I would have said anything to get him off.

He sat perched on my chest a few seconds longer, then grunted and rolled off. I sat up, gasping, rubbing my face where he had poked it.

"Sorry," Steve mumbled. "That was over the top. But I'm upset. It hurt, what Mr Crepsley said, and you ignoring me at school. You're my best friend, Darren, the only person I can really talk to. If you break up our friendship, I don't know what I'll do."

He started to cry. I watched him for a few seconds, torn between fear and sympathy. Then my nobler self got the better of me and I put an arm around his shoulder. "It's OK," I said. "I'll still be your friend. C'mon, Steve, quit crying, OK?"

He tried but it took a while for the tears to stop. "I must look a right fool," he finally sniffed.

"Nonsense," I said. "*I'm* the fool. I should have stood by you. I was a coward. I never stopped to imagine what you must be going through. I was only thinking of myself and Madam— " I pulled a face and stopped talking.

Steve stared at me curiously. "What were you going to say?" he asked.

"Nothing," I said. "It was a slip of the tongue."

He grunted. "You're a bad liar, Shan. Always were. Tell me what it was you were about to let slip."

I studied his face, wondering if I should tell him. I knew I shouldn't, that it could only mean trouble, but I felt sorry for him. Besides, I needed to tell someone. I wanted to show off my wonderful pet and the great tricks we could do.

"Can you keep a secret?" I asked.

"Of course," he snorted.

"This is a big one. You can't tell anyone, OK? If I tell you, it has to stay between the two of us. If you ever talk..."

"... *you'll* talk about me and Mr Crepsley," Steve said, grinning. "You have me over a barrel. No matter what you tell me, you know I can't grass, even if I wanted to. What's the big secret?"

"Wait a minute," I said. I got off the bed and opened the door to the room. "Mum?" I shouted.

"Yes?" came her muffled reply.

"I'm showing Steve my flute," I yelled. "I'm going to teach him how to play it, but only if we're not disturbed, OK?"

"OK," she called back.

I closed the door and smiled at Steve. He looked puzzled. "A flute?" he asked. "Your big secret is a flute?"

"That's part of it," I said. "Listen, do you remember Madam Octa? Mr Crepsley's spider?"

"Of course," he said. "I wasn't paying much attention to her when she was on but I don't think anyone could ever forget a creature like that. Those hairy legs: brrrr!"

I opened the door to the wardrobe while he was speaking and got out the cage. His eyes squinted when he saw it, then widened. "That's not what I think it is, is it?" he asked.

"That depends," I said, whipping off the cloth. "If you think it's a deadly performing spider — you're right!"

"Hell's bells!" he gasped, almost falling off the bed in shock. "That's a... she's a... where did... Wow!"

I was delighted with his reaction. I stood over the cage, smiling like a proud father. Madam Octa lay on the floor, quiet as ever, paying no attention to me or Steve.

"She's awesome!" Steve said, crawling closer for a better look. "She looks just the same as the one in the circus. I can't believe you found one that looks so similar. Where'd you get her? A pet shop? From a zoo?"

My smile slipped. "I got her from the Cirque Du Freak, of course," I said uneasily.

"From the freak show?" he asked, face crinkling. "They were selling live spiders? I didn't see any. How much did she cost?"

I shook my head and said: "I didn't buy her, Steve. I... Can't you guess? Don't you understand?"

"Understand what?" he asked.

"That's not a *similar* spider," I said. "That's the *same one*. It's Madam Octa."

He stared at me, as though he hadn't heard what I'd said. I was about to repeat, it but he spoke up before I could. "The... same ... one?" he asked in a slow, trembling voice.

"Yes," I said.

"You mean... that's... Madam Octa? *The* Madam Octa?"

"Yes," I said again, laughing at his shock.

"That's... Mr Crepsley's spider?"

"Steve, what's wrong? How many times do I have to say it for you to— "

"Wait a minute," he snapped, shaking his head. "If this is really Madam Octa, how did you get your hands on her? Did you find her outside? Did they sell her off?"

"Nobody would sell a great spider like this," I said.

"That's what I thought," Steve agreed. "So how did… " He left the question hanging in the air.

"I stole her," I said, puffing up proudly. "I went back to the theatre that Tuesday morning, crept in, found where she was and snuck out with her. I left a note telling Mr Crepsley not to come looking for her or I'd report his being a vampire to the police."

"You… you… " Steve was gasping. His face had turned white and he looked like he was about to collapse.

"Are you all right?" I asked.

"You… imbecile!" he roared. "You lunatic! You moron!"

"Hey!" I shouted, upset.

"Idiot! Dumbo! Cretin!" he yelled. "Do you realise what you've done? Have you any idea what sort of trouble you're in?"

"Huh?" I asked, bewildered.

"You stole a vampire's spider!" Steve shouted. "You stole from a member of the undead! What do you think he's going to do when he catches up with you, Darren? Spank your bottom and give you fifty lines? Tell your parents and make them ground you? We're talking about a *vampire*! He'll rip out your throat and feed you to the spider! He'll tear you to pieces and— "

"No, he won't," I said calmly.

"Of course he will," Steve replied.

"No," I said, "he *won't*. Because he won't find me. I stole the spider the Tuesday before last, so he's had nearly two whole weeks to track me down, but there hasn't been a sign of him. He left with the circus and won't ever come back, not if he knows what's good for him."

"I dunno," Steve said. "Vampires have long memories. He might return when you're grown up and with kids of your own."

"I'll worry about that when and if it happens," I said. "I've got away with it for the time being. I wasn't sure I would –

I thought he'd track me down and kill me – but I did. So quit with the names, all right?"

"You're something else," he laughed, shaking his head. "I thought *I* was daring, but stealing a vampire's pet! I never would have thought you had it in you. What made you do it?"

"I had to have her," I told him. "I saw her on stage and knew I'd do anything to get her. Then I discovered Mr Crepsley was a vampire and realised I could blackmail him. It's wrong, I know, but he's a vampire, so it's not *too* bad, is it? Stealing from someone bad: in a way it's a good thing, right?"

Steve laughed. "I don't know if it's good or bad," he said. "All I know is, if he ever comes looking for her, I wouldn't want to be in your shoes."

He studied the spider again. He stuck his face up close to the cage (but not close enough for her to strike him) and watched her belly bulging in and out.

"Have you let her out of the cage yet?" he asked.

"Every day," I said. I picked up the flute and gave a toot. Madam Octa jumped forward a couple of centimetres. Steve yelped and fell back on his bum. I howled with laughter.

"You can control her?" he gasped.

"I can make her do everything Mr Crepsley did," I said, trying not to sound boastful. "It's quite easy. She's perfectly safe as long as you concentrate. But if you let your thoughts wander for even a second… " I drew a finger across my throat and made a choking noise.

"Have you let her make a web over your lips?" Steve asked. His eyes were shining brightly.

"Not yet," I said. "I'm worried about letting her in my mouth: the thought of her slipping down my throat terrifies me. Besides, I'd need a partner to control her while she spun the web, and so far I've been alone."

"So far," Steve grinned, "but not any more." He got up and clapped his hands. "Let's do it. Teach me how to use that fancy tin whistle and let me at her. I'm not afraid to let her in my mouth. C'mon, let's go, let's go, let's go go go go GO!"

I couldn't ignore excitement like that. I knew it was unwise to involve Steve with the spider on such short notice – I should have made sure he got to know her better – but I ignored common sense and gave in to his wishes.

I told him he couldn't play the flute, not until he'd practised, but he could play with Madam Octa while I was controlling her. I ran him through the tricks we were going to do and made sure he understood everything.

"Being quiet is vital," I said. "Don't say anything. Don't even whistle loudly. Because if you disturb my attention and I lose control of her… "

"Yeah, yeah," Steve sighed. "I know. Don't worry. I can be quiet as a mouse when I want."

When he was ready, I unlocked Madam Octa's cage and began playing. She advanced at my order. I could hear Steve drawing in his breath, a little scared now that she was out in the open, but he gave no sign that he wanted to stop, so I went on blowing and started her off on her routine.

I let her do a lot of stuff by herself before allowing her near Steve. We'd developed a great understanding over the last week or so. The spider had grown used to my mind and the way it thought, and had learned to obey my commands almost before I finished sending them. I'd learned that she could work from the shortest of instructions: I only had to use a few words to prompt her into action.

Steve watched the show in total silence. He nearly clapped a few times but caught himself before his hands could meet and produce a noise. Instead of clapping, he gave me the thumbs-up sign and mouthed the words "Great", "Super", "Brilliant" and so on.

When the time came for Steve to take part in the act, I gave him the nod that we had agreed upon. He gulped, took a deep breath, then nodded back. He rose to his feet and stepped forward, keeping to the side so I wouldn't lose sight of Madam Octa. Then he sank to his knees and waited.

I played a new tune and sent a new set of orders. Madam Octa sat still, listening. When she knew what I wanted, she started creeping towards Steve. I saw him shivering and licking his lips. I was going to cancel the act and send the spider back to her cage, but then he stopped shaking and became calmer, so I continued.

He gave a small shudder when she started crawling up the leg of his trousers, but that was a natural response. I still got the shakes sometimes when I felt her hairy legs brushing against my skin.

I made Madam Octa crawl up the back of his neck and tickle his ears with her legs. He giggled softly and the last traces of his fear vanished. I felt more confident now that he was calmer, and so moved the spider round to the front of his face, where she built small cobwebs over his eyes and slid down his nose and bounced off his lips.

Steve was enjoying it and so was I. There were lots of new things I was able to do now that I had a partner.

She was on his right shoulder, preparing to slide down his arm, when the door opened and Annie walked in.

Normally Annie never enters my room before knocking. She's a great kid, not like other brats her age, and nearly always knocks politely and waits for a reply. But that evening, by sheer bad luck, she happened to barge in.

"Hey, Darren, where's my— " she started to say, then stopped.

113

She saw Steve and the monstrous spider on his shoulder, its fangs glinting as though getting ready to bite, and she did the natural thing.

She screamed.

The sound alarmed me. My head turned, the flute slid from my lips, and my concentration snapped. My link to Madam Octa disintegrated. She shook her head, took a couple of quick steps closer to Steve's throat, then bared her fangs and appeared to grin.

Steve roared with fear and surged to his feet. He swiped at the spider, but she ducked and his hand missed. Before he could try again, Madam Octa lowered her head, quick as a snake, and *sank her poison-tipped fangs deep into his neck!*

CHAPTER TWENTY-ONE

STEVE STIFFENED as soon as the spider bit him. His yells stopped dead in his throat, his lips turned blue, his eyes snapped wide open. For what seemed an eternity (though it couldn't have been more than three or four seconds), he tottered on his feet. Then he crumpled to the floor like a scarecrow.

The fall saved him. As with the goat at the Cirque Du Freak show, Madam Octa's first bite knocked Steve out, but didn't kill him straight off. I saw her moving along his neck before he fell, searching for the right spot, preparing for the second, killer bite.

The fall disturbed her. She slipped from Steve's neck and it took her a few seconds to climb back up.

Those seconds were all I needed.

I was in a state of shock, but the sight of her emerging over his shoulder like some terrible arachnid sunrise spurred me into life. I stooped for the flute, jammed it almost through the back of my throat, and blew the loudest note of my entire life.

"STOP!" I screamed inside my head, and Madam Octa leapt about half a metre into the air.

"Back inside the cage!" I commanded, and she hopped down from Steve's body and sped across the floor. As soon as she passed the bars of the door, I lunged forward and slammed it shut.

With Madam Octa taken care of, my attention turned to Steve. Annie was still screaming but I couldn't worry about her until I'd seen to my poisoned friend.

"Steve?" I asked, crawling close to his ear, praying for an answer. "Are you OK? Steve?" There was no reply. He was breathing, so I knew he was alive, but that was all. There was nothing else he could do. He couldn't talk or move his arms. He wasn't even able to blink.

I became aware of Annie standing behind me. She'd stopped screaming but I could feel her shaking.

"Is... is he... dead?" she asked in a tiny voice.

"Of course not!" I snapped. "You can see him breathing, can't you? Look at his belly and chest."

"But... why can't he move?" she asked.

"He's paralysed," I told her. "The spider injected him with poison which stops his limbs working. It's like putting him to sleep, except his brain's still active and he can see and hear everything."

I didn't know if this was true. I hoped it was. If the poison had left the heart and lungs alone, it might also have skipped his brain. But if it had got into his skull...

The thought was too terrible to consider.

"Steve, I'm going to help you up," I said. "I think if we move you around, the poison will wear off."

I stuck my arms around Steve's waist and hauled him to his feet. He was heavy but I took no notice of the weight. I dragged him around the room, shaking his arms and legs, talking to him as I went, telling him he was going to be all right, there wasn't enough poison in one bite to kill him, he would recover.

After ten minutes of this, there was no change and I was too tired to carry him any longer. I dropped him on the bed, then carefully arranged his body so he would be comfortable. His eyelids were open. They looked weird and were scaring me, so I closed them, but then he looked like a corpse, so I opened them again.

"Will he be all right?" Annie asked.

"Of course he will," I said, trying to sound positive. "The poison will wear off after a while and he'll be right as rain. It's only a matter of time."

I don't think she believed me but she said nothing, only sat on the edge of the bed and watched Steve's face like a hawk. I began wondering why Mum hadn't been up to investigate. I crept over to the open door and listened at the top of the stairs. I could hear the washing machine rumbling in the kitchen below. That explained it: our washing machine is old and clunky. You can't hear anything over the noise it makes if you're in the kitchen and it's turned on.

Annie was no longer on the bed when I returned. She was down on the floor, studying Madam Octa.

"It's the spider from the freak show, isn't it?" she asked.

"Yes," I admitted.

"The poisonous one?"

"Yes."

"How did you get it?" she asked.

"That's not important," I said, blushing.

"How did she get loose?" Annie asked.

"I let her out," I said.

"You *what*?!"

"It wasn't the first time," I told her. "I've had her for nearly two weeks. I've played with her lots of times. It's perfectly safe as long as there are no noises. If you hadn't come barging in when you did, she would have been— "

"No you don't," she growled. "You aren't laying the blame on me. Why didn't you tell me about her? If I'd known, I wouldn't have come busting in."

"I was going to," I said. "I was waiting until I was sure it was safe. Then Steve came and... " I couldn't continue.

I stuck the cage back in the wardrobe, where I wouldn't have to look at Madam Octa. I joined Annie by the bed and studied Steve's motionless form. We sat silently for almost an hour, just watching.

"I don't think he's going to recover," she finally said.

"Give it more time," I pleaded.

"I don't think time will help," she insisted. "If he was going to recover, he should be moving a bit by now."

"What do *you* know about it?" I asked roughly. "You're a child. You know nothing!"

"That's right," she agreed calmly. "But *you* don't know any more about it than me, do you?" I shook my head unhappily. "So stop pretending you do," she said.

She laid a hand on my arm and smiled bravely to show she wasn't trying to make me feel bad. "We have to tell Mum," she said. "We have to get her up here. She might know what to do."

"And if she doesn't?" I asked.

"Then we have to take him to a hospital," Annie said.

I knew she was right. I'd known it all along. I just didn't want to admit it.

"Let's give it another quarter of an hour," I said. "If he hasn't moved by then, we call her."

"A quarter of an hour?" she asked uncertainly.

"Not a minute more," I promised.

"OK," she agreed.

We sat in silence again and watched our friend. I thought about Madam Octa and how I was going to explain this to Mum.

To the doctors. To the *police!* Would they believe me when I told them Mr Crepsley was a vampire? I doubted it. They'd think I was lying. They might throw me in jail. They might say, since the spider was mine, I was to blame. They might charge me with murder and lock me away!

I checked my watch. Three minutes to go. No change in Steve.

"Annie, I need to ask a favour," I said.

She looked at me suspiciously. "What?"

"I don't want you to mention Madam Octa," I said.

"Are you crazy?" she shouted. "How else are you going to explain what's happened?"

"I don't know," I admitted. "I'll tell them I was out of the room. The bite marks are tiny. They look like small bee stings and are going down all the time. The doctors might not even notice them."

"We can't do that," Annie said. "They might need to examine the spider. They might— "

"Annie, if Steve dies, I'll be blamed," I said softly. "There are parts to this I can't tell you, that I can't tell anybody. All I can say is, if the worst happens, I'll be left carrying the can. Do you know what they do to murderers?"

"You're too young to be tried for murder," she said, but sounded uncertain.

"No, I'm not," I told her. "I'm too young to go to a real prison but they have special places for children. They'd hold me in one of those until I turned eighteen and then… Please, Annie." I started to cry. "I don't want to go to jail."

She started crying too. We held onto each other and sobbed like a couple of babies. "I don't want them to take you away," she wept. "I don't want to lose you."

"Then do you promise not to tell?" I asked. "Will you go back to your bedroom and pretend you saw and heard none of this?"

She nodded sadly. "But not if I think the truth can save him," she added. "If the doctors say they can't save him unless they find what bit him, I'm telling. OK?"

"OK," I agreed.

She got to her feet and headed for the door. She stopped in the middle of the room, turned, came back and kissed me on the forehead. "I love you, Darren," she said, "but you were a fool to bring that spider into this house, and if Steve dies, I think you *are* the one who should be blamed."

Then she ran from the room, sobbing.

I waited a few minutes, holding Steve's hand, begging him to recover, to show some sign of life. When my prayers weren't answered, I got to my feet, opened the window (to explain how the mystery attacker got in), took a deep breath, then ran downstairs, screaming for my mother.

CHAPTER TWENTY-TWO

THE AMBULANCE nurses asked my mother if Steve was diabetic or epileptic. She wasn't sure but didn't think so. They also asked about allergies and the like, but she explained that she wasn't his mother and didn't know.

I thought they'd take us with them in the ambulance, but they said there wasn't room. They got the number of Steve's phone and the name of his mum, but she wasn't home. One of the nurses asked my mother if she'd drive after them to hospital, to fill in as many of the forms as she could, so they could make a start. She agreed and bundled me and Annie into the car. Dad still wasn't home, so she rang him on his mobile to explain where we'd be. He said he'd come straight over.

That was a miserable ride. I sat in the back, trying not to meet Annie's eye, knowing I should tell the truth, but too afraid to. What made it even worse was, I knew if *I* was the one lying in a coma, Steve would own up immediately.

"What happened in there?" Mum asked over her shoulder. She was driving as fast as she could without breaking the speed limit, so wasn't able to look back at me. I was glad: I don't think I could have lied straight to her face.

"I'm not sure," I said. "We were chatting. Then I had to go to the toilet. When I got back…"

"You didn't see anything?" she asked.

"No," I lied, feeling my ears reddening with shame.

"I can't understand it," she muttered. "He felt so stiff and his skin was turning blue. I thought he was dead."

"I think he was bitten," Annie said. I nearly gave her a dig in the ribs, but at the last second remembered I was depending on her to keep my secret.

"Bitten?" Mum asked.

"There were a couple of marks on his neck," Annie said.

"I saw them," Mum said. "But I don't think that's it, dear."

"Why not?" Annie asked. "If a snake or a… *spider* got in and bit him…" She glanced over at me and blushed a little, recalling her promise.

"A spider?" Mum shook her head. "No, dear, spiders don't go around biting people and sending them into shock, not around here."

"So what was it?" Annie asked.

"I'm not sure," Mum replied. "Maybe he ate something that didn't agree with him, or had a heart attack."

"Children don't have heart attacks," Annie snorted.

"They do," Mum said. "It's rare, but it can happen. Still, the doctors will sort all that out. They know more about these things than we do."

I wasn't used to hospitals, so I spent some time looking around while Mum was filling in the forms. It was the whitest place I'd ever seen: white walls, white floors, white uniforms. It wasn't very busy but there was a buzz to the place, a sound of bed springs and coughing, machines humming, knives slicing, doctors speaking softly.

We didn't say much while sitting there. Mum said Steve had

been admitted and was being examined but it might be a while before they discovered what was wrong. "They sounded optimistic," she said.

Annie was thirsty, so Mum sent me with her to get drinks from the machine round the corner. Annie glanced around while I was putting in the coins, to make sure nobody could overhear.

"How long are you going to wait?" she asked.

"Until I hear what they have to say," I told her. "We'll let them examine him. Hopefully they'll know what sort of poison it is and be able to cure him by themselves."

"And if they can't?" she asked.

"Then I tell them," I promised.

"What if he dies before that?" she asked softly.

"He won't," I said.

"But what if— "

"He won't!" I snapped. "Don't talk like that. Don't even *think* like that. We have to hope for the best. We must believe he will pull through. Mum and Dad have always told us good thoughts help make sick people better, haven't they? He needs us to believe in him."

"He needs the truth more," she grumbled, but let the matter drop. We took the drinks back to the bench and drank in silence.

Dad arrived not long after, still in his work clothes. He kissed Mum and Annie and squeezed my shoulder manfully. His dirty hands left grease marks on my T-shirt, but that didn't bother me.

"Any news?" he asked.

"None yet," Mum said. "They're examining him. It could be hours before we hear anything."

"What happened to him, Angela?" Dad asked.

"We don't know yet," Mum said. "We'll have to wait and see."

"I hate waiting," Dad grumbled, but since he had no other choice, he had to, the same as the rest of us.

Nothing further happened for a couple of hours, until Steve's mum arrived. Her face was white like Steve's, and her lips were pinched together. She made straight for me, grabbed me by the shoulders and shook me hard. "What have you done to him?" she screeched. "Have you hurt my boy? Have you killed my Steve?"

"Here! Stop that!" Dad gasped.

Steve's mum ignored him. "What have you done?" she screamed again, and shook me even harder. I tried to say "Nothing" but my teeth were clattering. "What have you done? What have you done?" she repeated, then suddenly stopped shaking me, let go and collapsed to the floor, where she bawled like a baby.

Mum got off the bench and crouched beside Mrs Leonard. She stroked the back of her head and whispered kind words to her, then helped her up and sat down with her. Mrs Leonard was still crying, and was now moaning about what a bad mother she'd been and how much Steve hated her.

"You two go and play somewhere else," Mum said to Annie and me. We started away. "Darren," Mum called me back. "Don't take any notice of what she was saying. She doesn't blame you. She's just afraid."

I nodded miserably. What would Mum say if she knew Mrs Leonard was right and I *was* to blame?

Annie and me found a couple of arcade games which kept us busy. I didn't think I'd be able to play but after a few minutes I forgot about Steve and the hospital and got caught up in the games. It was nice to slip away from the worries of the real world for a while, and if I hadn't run out of coins, I might have stayed there all night.

When we returned to our chairs, Mrs Leonard had calmed down and was off with Mum, filling out forms. Annie and me sat and the waiting began all over again.

Annie began yawning about ten o'clock and that set me off too. Mum took one look at us and ordered us home. I started to argue but she cut me short.

"You can't do any good here," she said. "I'll ring as soon as I hear anything, even if it's the middle of the night, OK?"

I hesitated. This would be my final chance to mention the spider. I came very close to spilling the beans, but I was tired and couldn't find the words. "OK," I said glumly, then left.

Dad drove us home. I wondered what he'd do if I told him about the spider, Mr Crepsley and the rest. He would have punished me, I'm sure, but that's not why I didn't tell him: I kept quiet because I knew he'd be ashamed of the way I'd lied and put my own well-being before Steve's. I was afraid he'd hate me.

Annie was asleep by the time we got home. Dad lifted her in from the back seat and took her to bed. I walked slowly up to my room and got undressed. I kept cursing myself under my breath.

Dad looked in as I was putting my clothes away. "Will you be OK?" he asked. I nodded. "Steve will recover," he said. "I'm sure of it. The doctors know their stuff. They'll bring him round."

I nodded again, not trusting myself to answer. Dad stood in the doorway a moment longer, then sighed, left, and stomped downstairs to his study.

I was hanging my trousers up in the wardrobe when I noticed Madam Octa's cage. Slowly, I pulled it out. She was lying in the middle, breathing easily, calm as ever.

I studied the colourful spider and wasn't impressed by what I saw. She was bright, yes, but ugly and hairy and nasty. I began to hate her. She was the real villain, the one who bit Steve for no good reason. I had fed her and cared for her and played with her. This was how she repaid me.

"You bloody monster!" I snarled, shaking the cage. "You ungrateful creep!"

I gave the cage another shake. Her legs gripped the bars tightly. This made me madder and I yanked the cage roughly from side to side, trying to make her lose her grip, hoping to hurt her.

I spun about in a circle, whirling the cage around by the handle. I was cursing, calling her every name under the sun, wishing she was dead, wishing I'd never set eyes on her, wishing I had the guts to take her out of the cage and squeeze her to death.

Finally, as my rage reached bursting point, I hurled the cage as far away from me as possible. I wasn't looking where I was throwing, and got a shock when I saw it sail through the open window and out into the night.

I watched it flying away, then hurried after it. I was scared it would hit the ground and break open, because I knew if the doctors weren't able to save Steve by themselves, they might be able to with the help of Madam Octa: if they studied her, they might find out how to cure him. But if she escaped...

I rushed to the window. I was too late to grab for the cage but at least I could see where it landed. I watched as it floated out and down, praying it wouldn't break. It seemed to take ages to fall.

Just before it hit the ground, a hand darted out from the shadows of the night and snatched it from the air.

A hand?!?

I leaned forward quickly for a better view. It was a dark night and at first I couldn't see who was down there. But then the person stepped forward and all was revealed.

First, I saw his wrinkly hands holding the cage. Then his long red clothes. Then his cropped orange hair. Then his long ugly scar. And, finally, his sharp toothy grin.

It was *Mr Crepsley.* The *vampire.*

And he was smiling up at me!

CHAPTER TWENTY-THREE

I STOOD by the window, expecting him to turn into a bat and come flying up, but he did nothing apart from shake the cage gently to make sure Madam Octa was all right.

Then, still smiling, he turned and walked away. Within a matter of seconds he had been swallowed from sight by the night.

I shut the window and fled to the safety of my bed, where my mind turned inside-out with questions. How long had he been down there? If he knew where Madam Octa was, why hadn't he taken her before this? I thought he'd be furious, but he seemed amused. Why hadn't he ripped out my throat like Steve said he would?

Sleep was impossible. I was more terrified now than I had been the night after stealing the spider. Back then I could tell myself that he didn't know who I was and so couldn't find me.

I thought about telling Dad. After all, a vampire knew where we lived and had reason to bear a grudge against us. Dad should know. He should be warned and given a chance to prepare a defence. But...

He wouldn't believe me. Especially not now that Madam

Octa was gone. I imagined trying to convince him that vampires were real, that one had been to our house and might come back. He'd think I was a nutter.

I was able to snooze a bit when dawn rolled round, because I knew the vampire couldn't launch an attack until sunset. It wasn't much of a sleep, but even a small bit of rest did me good and I was able to think clearly when I woke. I realised, as I thought it over, that I had no reason to be afraid. If the vampire had wanted to kill me, he could have done it last night when I was unprepared. For some reason, he didn't want me dead, at least not yet.

With that worry off my mind, I could focus on Steve and my real problem: whether to reveal the truth or not. Mum had stayed at the hospital all night, taking care of Mrs Leonard, ringing round to let friends and neighbours know of Steve's illness. If she had been home, I might have told her, but the thought of telling Dad filled me with dread.

Ours was a very quiet house that Sunday. Dad cooked eggs and sausages for breakfast, and burned them as he normally does when he cooks, but we didn't complain. I hardly even tasted the food as I gulped it down. I wasn't hungry. The only reason I ate was to pretend it was any other average Sunday.

Mum rang as we were finishing. She had a long talk with Dad. He didn't say much, only nodded and grunted. Annie and I sat still, trying to hear what was being said. He came in and sat down when he was finished talking.

"How is he?" I asked.

"Not good," Dad said. "The doctors don't know what to make of it. It seems Annie was right: it is poison. But not like any they know. They've sent samples to experts in other hospitals, and hopefully one of them will know more about it. But... " He shook his head.

"Will he die?" Annie asked quietly.

"Maybe," Dad said, being honest. I was glad of that. All too often adults lie to kids about serious matters. I'd rather know the truth about death than be lied to.

Annie started to cry. Dad picked her up and perched her on his lap. "Hey, now, there's no need to cry," he said. "It's not over yet. He's still alive. He's breathing and his brain doesn't seem to have been affected. If they can figure out a way to fight the poison in his body, he should be fine."

"How long does he have?" I asked.

Dad shrugged. "The way he is, they could keep him alive for ages with machines."

"You mean like someone in a coma?" I asked.

"Exactly."

"How long before they have to start using machines?" I asked.

"A few days, they think," Dad answered. "They can't say for sure, seeing as how they don't know what they're dealing with, but they think it will be a couple of days before his respiratory and coronary systems begin to shut down."

"His what?" Annie asked between sobs.

"His lungs and heart," Dad explained. "As long as those are working, he's alive. They have to use a drip to feed him but otherwise he's OK. It's when — *if* — he stops breathing by himself that the trouble really begins."

A couple of days. It wasn't much. The day before, he'd had a whole lifetime to look forward to. Now he had a couple of days.

"Can I go see him?" I asked.

"This afternoon, if you feel up to it," Dad said.

"I'll feel up to it," I vowed.

The hospital was busier this time, packed with visitors. I'd never seen so many boxes of chocolates and flowers. Everybody seemed to be carrying one or the other. I wanted to buy something for Steve at the hospital shop but had no money.

I expected Steve to be on the children's ward but he was in a room by himself, because the doctors wanted to study him, and also because they weren't sure if what he had was catching. We had to wear masks and gloves and long green gowns when we entered.

Mrs Leonard was asleep in a chair. Mum made a sign for us to be quiet. She gave us a hug, one by one, then spoke to Dad.

"A couple of results have come in from other hospitals," she told him, her voice muffled by the mask. "All negative."

"Surely *someone* knows what this is," Dad said. "How many different types of poison can there be?"

"Thousands," she said. "They've sent specimens to foreign hospitals. Hopefully one of them will have a record of it, but it's going to be some time before they get back to us."

I studied Steve while they were talking. He was tucked neatly into the bed. A drip was attached to one arm, and wires and stuff to his chest. There were needle marks where doctors had taken samples of his blood. His face was white and stiff. He looked terrible!

I started crying and couldn't stop. Mum put her arms around me and hugged me tight, but that only made it worse. I tried telling her about the spider but I was crying too much for my words to be heard. Mum kept hugging and kissing and shushing me, and eventually I quit trying.

New visitors arrived, relatives of Steve's, and Mum decided to leave them alone with him and his mother. She led us out, removed my mask and wiped the tears from my face with a tissue.

"There," she said. "That's better." She smiled and tickled me until I grinned back. "He'll be OK," she promised. "I know he looks bad, but the doctors are doing all they can. We have to trust them and hope for the best, OK?"

"OK," I sighed.

"I thought he looked quite good," Annie said, squeezing my hand. I smiled thankfully at her.

"Are you coming home now?" Dad asked Mum.

"I'm not sure," she said. "I think I should stick around a little longer in case— "

"Angela, you've done enough for the time being," Dad said firmly. "I bet you didn't get any sleep last night, did you?"

"Not much," Mum admitted.

"And if you stay on now, you won't get any today either. Come on, Angie, let's go." Dad calls Mum "Angie" when he's trying to sweet-talk her into something. "There are other people who can look after Steve and his mum. Nobody expects you to do everything."

"All right," she agreed. "But I'm coming back tonight to see if they need me."

"Fair enough," he said, and led the way out to the car. It hadn't been much of a visit but I didn't complain. I was glad to get away.

I thought about Steve as we drove home, how he looked and *why* he looked that way. I thought about the poison in his veins and felt pretty sure the doctors would fail to cure it. I bet no doctor in the world had ever come across poison from a spider like Madam Octa before.

However bad Steve had looked today, I knew he'd look a lot worse after another couple. I imagined him hooked up to a breathing machine, his face covered with a mask, tubes sticking into him. It was a horrible thought.

There was only one way to save Steve. Only one person who might know about the poison and how to beat it.

Mr Crepsley.

As we pulled into the drive back home and got out of the car, I made up my mind: I was going to track him down and make him do what he could to help Steve. As soon as it got dark, I'd sneak out and find the vampire, wherever he might be. And if I couldn't force it out of him and come back with a cure...

...I wouldn't come back at all.

CHAPTER TWENTY-FOUR

I HAD to wait until nearly eleven o'clock. I would have gone earlier, while Mum was at the hospital, but a couple of Dad's pals came round with kids of their own and I had to play host.

Mum returned home about ten. She was tired, so Dad quickly cleared the house of visitors. They had a cup of tea and a chat in the kitchen, then went up to bed. I let them drift off to sleep, then snuck downstairs and let myself out the back door.

I sped through the dark like a comet. Nobody saw or heard me, I moved so fast. I had a cross in one pocket, which I'd found in Mum's jewellery box, and a bottle of holy water in the other, which one of Dad's pen friends had sent to us years ago. I wasn't able to find a stake. I'd thought about bringing a sharp knife instead, but probably would only have cut myself. I'm clumsy with knives.

The old theatre was pitch black and deserted. I used the front door this time.

I didn't know what I'd do if the vampire wasn't here, but somehow I sensed he would be. It was like the day Steve threw the scraps of paper up in the air with the winning ticket hidden amongst them, and I shut my eyes and reached out blindly. It was *destiny*.

It took a while to find the cellar. I'd brought a torch but the battery was almost dead and it flickered out after a couple of minutes, leaving me to grope through the dark like a mole. When I did find the steps, I started straight down, not giving fear time to catch up.

The further down I went, the brighter it got, until I reached the bottom and saw five tall flickering candles. I was surprised – weren't vampires supposed to be afraid of fire? – but glad.

Mr Crepsley was waiting for me at the other end of the cellar. He was sitting at a small table, playing a game of cards with himself.

"Good morning, Master Shan," he said, without looking up.

I cleared my throat before replying. "It's not morning," I said. "It's the middle of the night."

"To me, that is morning," he said, then looked up and grinned. His teeth were long and sharp. This was the closest to him I'd been and I expected to spot all sorts of details – red teeth, long ears, narrow eyes – but he looked like a normal human, albeit a tremendously ugly one.

"You've been waiting for me, haven't you?" I asked.

"Yes," he nodded.

"How long have you known where Madam Octa was?"

"I found her the night you stole her," he said.

"Why didn't you take her then?"

He shrugged. "I was going to, but I got to thinking about the sort of boy who would dare steal from a vampire, and I decided you might be worth further study."

"Why?" I asked, trying to stop my knees from knocking together.

"Why indeed?" he replied mockingly. He clicked his fingers and the cards on the table jumped together and slid back into the packet by themselves. He put it away and cracked his knuckles.

"Tell me, Darren Shan, why have you come? Is it to steal from me again? Do you still desire Madam Octa?"

I shook my head. "I never want to see that monster again!" I snarled.

He laughed. "She will be so sad to hear that."

"Don't make fun of me," I warned him. "I don't like being teased."

"No?" he asked. "And what will you do if I continue?"

I pulled out the cross and bottle of holy water and held them up. "I'll strike you with these!" I roared, expecting him to fall back, frozen with fear. But he didn't. Instead he smiled, clicked his fingers again, and suddenly the cross and plastic bottle were no longer in my hands. They were in *his*.

He studied the cross, chuckled and squeezed it into a little ball, as though it was made of tinfoil. Next he uncorked the holy water and drank it.

"You know what I love?" he asked. "I love people who watch lots of horror movies and read horror books. Because they believe what they read and hear, and come packing silly things like crosses and holy water, instead of weapons which could do real damage, like guns and hand grenades."

"You mean… crosses don't… hurt you?" I stammered.

"Why should they?" he asked.

"Because you're… evil," I said.

"Am I?" he asked.

"Yes," I said. "You must be. You're a vampire. Vampires are evil."

"You should not believe everything you are told," he said. "It is true that our appetites are rather exotic. But just because we drink blood does not mean that we are evil. Are vampire bats evil when they drink the blood of cows and horses?"

"No," I said. "But that's different. They're animals."

"Humans are animals too," he told me. "If a vampire kills

a human, then yes, he is evil. But one who just takes a little blood to fill his rumbling belly... Where is the harm in that?"

I couldn't answer. I was numb and no longer knew what to believe. I was at his mercy, alone and defenceless.

"I see you are not in the mood for a debate," he said. "Very well. I will save the speeches for another time. So tell me, Darren Shan: what is it you want if not my spider?"

"She bit Steve Leonard," I told him.

"The one known as Steve Leopard," he said, nodding. "A nasty business. Still, little boys who play with things they do not understand can hardly complain if— "

"I want you to make him better!" I yelled, interrupting.

"*I?*" he asked, acting surprised. "But I am not a doctor. I am not a specialist. I am just a circus performer. A freak. Remember?"

"No," I said. "You're more. I know you can save him. I know you have the power."

"Maybe," he said. "Madam Octa's bite is deadly, but for every poison there exists an antidote. Maybe I do have the cure. Maybe I have a bottle of serum which will restore your friend's natural physical functions."

"Yes!" I shouted gleefully. "I knew it! I knew it! I— "

"But maybe," Mr Crepsley said, raising a long bony finger to silence me, "it is a small bottle. Maybe there is only a tiny amount of serum. Maybe it is very precious. Maybe I want to save it for a real emergency, in case Madam Octa ever bites *me*. Maybe I do not want to waste it on an evil little brat."

"No," I said softly. "You have to give it to me. You have to use it on Steve. He's dying. You can't let him die."

"I most certainly can," Mr Crepsley laughed. "What is your friend to me? You heard him the night he was here: he said he would become a vampire hunter when he grew up!"

"He didn't mean it," I gasped. "He only said that because he was angry."

"Perhaps," Mr Crepsley mused, tugging at his chin and stroking his scar. "But again, I ask: why should I save Steve Leopard? The serum was expensive and cannot be replaced."

"I can pay for it," I cried, and that was what he had been waiting for. I saw it in his eyes, the way they narrowed, the way he hunched forward, smiling. This was why he hadn't taken Madam Octa that first night. This was why he hadn't left town.

"Pay for it?" he asked slyly. "But you are only a boy. You cannot possibly have enough money to buy the cure."

"I'll pay in bits," I promised. "Every week for fifty years, or as long as you want. I'll get a job when I grow up and give you all my money. I swear."

He shook his head. "No," he said softly. "Your money does not interest me."

"What *does* interest you?" I asked in a low voice. "I'm sure you have a price. That's why you waited for me, isn't it?"

"You are a clever young man," he said. "I knew that when I woke up to find my spider gone and your note in her place. I said to myself, 'Larten, there goes a most remarkable child, a true prodigy. There goes a boy who is going places'."

"Quit with the bull and tell me what you want," I snarled.

He laughed nastily, then grew serious. "You remember what Steve Leopard and I talked about?" he asked.

"Of course," I replied. "He wanted to become a vampire. You said he was too young, so he said he'd become your assistant. That was all right by you, but then you found out he was evil, so you said no."

"That about sums it up," he agreed. "Except, if you recall, I was not too keen on the idea of an assistant. They can be useful but also a burden."

"Where's all this leading?" I asked.

"I have had a rethink since then," he said. "I decided it might not be such a bad thing after all, especially now that I have been separated from the Cirque Du Freak and will have to fend for myself. An assistant could be just what the witch doctor ordered." He smiled at his little joke.

I frowned. "You mean you'll let Steve become your assistant now?"

"Heavens, no!" he yelped. "That monster? There is no telling what he will do as he matures. No, Darren Shan, I do not want Steve Leopard to be my assistant." He pointed at me with his long bony finger again, and I knew what he was going to say seconds before he said it.

"You want *me*!" I sighed, beating him to the punch, and his dark, sinister smile told me I was right.

CHAPTER TWENTY-FIVE

"YOU'RE CRAZY!" I yelled, stumbling backwards. "There's no way I'd become your assistant! You must be mad to even think such a thing!"

Mr Crepsley shrugged. "Then Steve Leopard dies," he said simply.

I stopped retreating. "Please," I begged, "there must be another way."

"The issue is not open to debate," he said. "If you wish to save your friend, you must join me. If you refuse, we have nothing further to discuss."

"What if I— "

"Do not waste my time!" he snapped, pounding on the table. "I have lived in this dirty hole for two weeks, putting up with fleas and cockroaches and lice. If you are not interested in my offer, say so and I will leave. But do not waste my time with other options, because there are none."

I nodded slowly and took a few steps forward. "Tell me more about being a vampire's assistant," I said.

He smiled. "You will be my travelling companion," he explained. "You will travel with me across the world. You will be my eyes and hands during the day. You will guard me while I sleep. You will find food for me if it is scarce. You will take my clothes to the laundry. You will polish my shoes. You will look after Madam Octa. In short, you will see to my every need. In return, I will teach you the ways of the vampires."

"Do I *have* to become a vampire?" I asked.

"Eventually," he said. "At first you will only have some vampire powers. I will make you a half-vampire. That means you will be able to move about during the day. You will not need much blood to keep you ticking over. You will have certain powers but not all. And you will only age at a fifth the regular rate, instead of the full vampire's tenth."

"What does that mean?" I asked, confused.

"Vampires do not live forever," he explained, "but we do live far longer than humans. We age about one-tenth the regular rate. Which means, for every ten years that pass, we age one. As a half-vampire, you will age one year for every five."

"You mean, for every five years that pass, I'll only be one year older?" I asked.

"That is right."

"I dunno," I muttered. "It sounds dodgy to me."

"It is your choice," he said. "I cannot force you to become my assistant. If you decide it is not to your liking, you are free to leave."

"But Steve will die if I do that!" I cried.

"Yes," he agreed. "It is your assistance or his life."

"That's not much of a choice," I grumbled.

"No," he admitted, "it is not. But it is the only one on offer. Do you accept?"

I thought it over. I wanted to say no, run away and never return. But if I did, Steve would die. Was he worth such a deal? Did I feel guilty enough to offer my life for his? The answer was:

Yes.

"OK," I sighed. "I don't like it, but my hands are tied. I just want you to know this: if I ever get the chance to betray you, I will. If the opportunity arises to pay you back, I'll take it. You'll never be able to trust me."

"Fair enough," he said.

"I mean it," I warned him.

"I know you do," he said. "That is why I want you. A vampire's assistant must have spirit. Your fighting quality is exactly what drew me to you. You will be a dangerous lad to have around, I am sure, but in a fight, when the chips are down, I am just as sure you will be a worthy ally."

I took a deep breath. "How do we do it?" I asked.

He stood and pushed the table aside. Stepped forward until he was about half a metre away. He seemed tall as a building. There was a foul smell to him that I hadn't noticed before, the smell of *blood*.

He raised his right hand and showed me the back of it. His nails weren't especially long but they looked sharp. He raised his left hand and pressed the nails of the right into the fleshy tips of his left-hand fingers. Then he used his other set of nails to mark the right-hand fingers in the same way. He winced as he did it.

"Lift your hands," he grunted. I was watching the blood drip from his fingers and didn't obey the command. "Now!" he yelled, grabbing my hands and jerking them up.

He dug his nails into the soft tips of my fingers, all ten of them at once. I cried out with pain and fell back, tucking my hands in at my sides, rubbing them against my jacket.

"Do not be such a baby," he jeered, tugging my hands free.

"It hurts!" I howled.

"Of course it does," he laughed. "It hurt me too. Did you think becoming a vampire was easy? Get used to the pain. Much of it lies ahead."

He put a couple of my fingers in his mouth and sucked some blood out. I watched as he rolled it around his mouth, testing it. Finally he nodded and swallowed. "It is good blood," he said. "We can proceed."

He pressed his fingers against mine, wound to wound. For a few seconds there was a numb feeling at the ends of my arms. Then I felt a gushing sensation and realised my blood was moving from my body to his through my left hand, while his blood was entering mine through my right.

It was a strange, tingling feeling. I felt his blood travel up my right arm, then down the side of my body and over to the left. When it reached my heart there was a stabbing pain and I nearly collapsed. The same thing was happening to Mr Crepsley and I could see him grinding his teeth and sweating.

The pain lasted until Mr Crepsley's blood crept down my left arm and started flowing back into his body. We remained joined a couple more seconds, until he broke free with a shout. I fell backwards to the floor. I was dizzy and felt sick.

"Give me your fingers," Mr Crepsley said. I looked across and saw him licking his. "My spit will heal the wounds. You will lose all your blood and die otherwise."

I glanced down at my hands and saw blood leaking out. Stretching them forth, I let the vampire put them in his mouth and run his rough tongue over the tips.

When he released them, the flow had stopped. I wiped the leftover blood off on a rag. I studied my fingers and noted they now had ten tiny scars running across them.

"That is how you recognise a vampire," Mr Crepsley told me. "There are other ways to change a human but the fingers are the simplest and least painful method."

"Is that it?" I asked. "Am I a half-vampire now?"

"Yes," he said.

"I don't feel any different," I told him.

"It will take a few days for the effects to become apparent," he said. "There is always a period of adjustment. The shock would be too great otherwise."

"How do you become a full vampire?" I asked.

"The same way," he said, "only you stay joined longer, so more of the vampire's blood enters your body."

"What will I be able to do with my new powers?" I asked. "Will I be able to change into a bat?"

His laughter rocked the room. "A bat!" he shrieked. "You do not believe those silly stories, do you? How on Earth could somebody the size of you or I turn into a tiny flying rat? Use your brain, boy. We can no more turn into bats, rats or fog than we can turn into ships, planes or monkeys!"

"So what can we do?" I asked.

He scratched his chin. "There is too much to explain right now," he said. "We must tend to your friend. If he does not get the antidote before tomorrow morning, the serum will not work. Besides, we have plenty of time to discuss secret powers." He grinned. "You could say we have all the time in the world."

CHAPTER TWENTY-SIX

MR CREPSLEY led the way up the stairs and out of the building. He walked confidently through the darkness. I thought I could see a bit better than I could when coming in, but that might just have been because my eyes were used to the dark, not because of the vampire blood in my veins.

Once outside, he told me to hop up on his back. "Keep your arms wrapped around my neck," he said. "Do not let go or make any sudden movements."

As I was getting up, I looked down and saw he was wearing slippers. I thought it was strange but didn't say anything.

When I was on his back, he started running. I didn't notice anything odd at first, but soon began to realise how fast buildings were zipping by. Mr Crepsley's legs didn't seem to be moving that quickly. Instead, it was as if the world was moving faster and we were slipping past it!

We reached the hospital in a couple of minutes. Normally it would have taken twenty minutes, and that was if you sprinted all the way.

"How did you do that?" I asked, sliding down.

"Speed is relative," he said, tugging his red cloak tight around

144

his shoulders, pulling back into the shadows so we could not be seen, and that was all the answer he gave.

"Which room is your friend in?" he asked.

I told him Steve's room number. He looked up, counting windows, then nodded and told me to hop back up on his back. When I was in position, he walked over to the wall, took off his slippers and laid his fingers and toes against the wall. Then he shoved his nails forward, into the brick!

"Hmmm," he muttered. "It is crumbly but it will hold us. Do not panic if we slip. I know how to land on my feet. It takes a very long fall to kill a vampire."

He climbed up the wall, digging his nails in, moving a hand forward, then a foot, then the other hand and foot, one after the other. He moved quickly and within moments we were at Steve's window, crouching on the ledge, gazing in.

I wasn't sure of the time, but it was very late. Nobody was in the room apart from Steve. Mr Crepsley tried the window. It was locked. He laid the fingers of one hand beside the glass covering the latch, then clicked the fingers of his other hand.

The latch sprang open! He shoved the window up and stepped inside. I got down from his back. While he checked the door, I examined Steve. His breathing was more ragged than it had been and there were new tubes all over his body, hooked up to menacing-looking machines.

"The poison has worked rapidly," Mr Crepsley said, gazing down at him over my shoulder. "We might be too late to save him." I felt my insides turn to ice at his words.

Mr Crepsley bent over and rolled up one of Steve's eyelids. For a few long seconds he stared at the eyeball and held Steve's right-hand wrist. Finally he grunted.

"We are in time," he said, and I felt my heart lifting. "But it is a good job you did not wait any longer. A few more hours and he would have been a goner."

"Just get on with it and cure him," I snapped, not wanting to know how close to death my best friend had come.

Mr Crepsley reached into one of his many pockets and produced a small glass vial. He turned on the bedside lamp and held the bottle up to the light to examine the serum. "I must be careful," he told me. "This antidote is almost as lethal as the poison. A couple of drops too many and… " He didn't need to finish.

He tilted Steve's head to one side and told me to hold it that way. He leaned one of his nails against the flesh of Steve's neck and made a small cut. Blood oozed out. He stuck his finger over it, then removed the cork of the bottle with his other hand.

He lifted the vial to his mouth and prepared to drink. "What are you doing?" I asked.

"It must be passed on by mouth," he said. "A doctor could inject it but I do not know about needles and the like."

"Is that safe?" I asked. "Won't you pass on germs?"

Mr Crepsley grinned. "If you want to call a doctor, feel free," he said. "Otherwise, have some faith in a man who was doing this long before your grandfather was born."

He poured the serum into his mouth, then rolled it from side to side. He leaned forward and covered the cut with his lips. His cheeks bulged out, then in, as he blew the serum into Steve.

He sat back when he was finished and wiped around his mouth. He spat the last of the fluid onto the floor. "I am always afraid of swallowing that stuff by accident," he said. "One of these nights, I am going to take a course and learn how to do this the easy way."

I was about to reply, but then Steve moved. His neck flexed, then his head, then his shoulders. His arms twitched and his legs started to jerk. His face creased up and he began to moan.

"What's happening?" I asked, afraid that something had gone wrong.

"It is all right," Mr Crepsley said, putting away the bottle. "He was on the brink of death. The journey back is never a pleasant one. He will be in pain for some time, but he will live."

"Will there be any side effects?" I asked. "He won't be paralysed from the waist down or anything?"

"No," Mr Crepsley said. "He will be fine. He will feel a bit stiff and will catch colds very easily, but otherwise he will be the same as he was before."

Steve's eyes shot open suddenly and focused on me and Mr Crepsley. A puzzled look swept across his face and he tried speaking. But his mouth wouldn't work, and then his eyes went blank and closed again.

"Steve?" I called, shaking him. "Steve?"

"That is going to happen a lot," Mr Crepsley said. "He will be slipping in and out of consciousness all night. By morning he should be awake and by afternoon he will be sitting up and asking for dinner.

"Come," he said. "Let us go."

"I want to stick around a while longer, to make sure he recovers," I replied.

"You mean you want to make sure I have not tricked you," Mr Crepsley laughed. "We will come back tomorrow and you will see that he is fine. We really must go now. If we stay any— "

All of a sudden, the door opened and a nurse walked in!

"What's going on here?" she shouted, stunned to see us. "Who the hell are— "

Mr Crepsley reacted quickly, grabbed Steve's bed covers and threw them over the nurse. She fell down as she tried to remove the sheets, getting her hands stuck in their folds.

"Come," Mr Crepsley hissed, rushing to the window. "We have to leave immediately."

I stared at the hand he was holding out, then at Steve, then at the nurse, then at the open door.

Mr Crepsley lowered his hand. "I see," he said in a bleak voice. "You are going to go back on our deal." I hesitated, opened my mouth to say something, then — acting without thinking — turned and made a dash for the door!

I thought he would stop me, but he did nothing, only howled after me as I ran: "Very well. Run, Darren Shan! It will do you no good. You are a creature of the night now. You are one of us! You will be back. You will come crawling on your knees, begging for help. Run, fool, run!"

And he began to laugh.

His laughter followed me through the corridor, down the stairs and out the front door. I kept glancing over my shoulder as I ran, expecting him to swoop down on me, but there was no sign of him on the way home, not a glimpse or a smell or a sound.

All that remained of him was his laughter, which echoed through my brain like a witch's cackling curse.

CHAPTER TWENTY-SEVEN

I ACTED surprised when Mum got off the phone that Monday morning and told me Steve had recovered. She was excited and did a little dance with me and Annie in the kitchen.

"He snapped out of it by himself?" Dad asked.

"Yes," she said. "The doctors can't understand it, but nobody's complaining."

"Incredible," Dad muttered.

"Maybe it's a miracle," Annie said and I had to turn my head aside to hide my smile. Some miracle!

While Mum set off to see Mrs Leonard, I started out for school. I was half-afraid the sunlight would burn me when I left the house, but of course it didn't. Mr Crepsley had told me I would be able to move about during the day.

I wondered, from time to time, if it had been a bad dream. It seemed crazy, looking back. Deep down I knew it was real, but I tried believing otherwise, and sometimes almost did.

The part I hated most was the thought of being stuck in this body for so long. How would I explain it to Mum and Dad and everybody else? I'd look silly after a couple of years, especially at school, stuck in a class with people who looked older than me.

I went to visit Steve on Tuesday. He was sitting up, watching TV, eating a box of chocolates. He was delighted to see me and told me about his stay in hospital, the food, the games nurses brought him to play with, the presents that were piling up.

"I'll have to get bitten by poisonous spiders more often," he joked.

"I wouldn't make a habit of it if I were you," I told him. "You might not get well next time."

He studied me thoughtfully. "You know, the doctors are baffled," he said. "They don't know what made me sick and they don't know how I recovered."

"You didn't tell them about Madam Octa?" I asked.

"No," he said. "There didn't seem much point. It would have meant trouble for you."

"Thanks."

"What happened to her?" he asked. "What did you do with her after she bit me?"

"I killed her," I lied. "I got mad and stomped her to death."

"Really?" he asked.

"Really."

He nodded slowly, never taking his eyes off me. "When I first woke up," he said, "I thought I saw *you*. I must have been mistaken, because it was the middle of the night. But it was a life-like dream. I even thought I saw someone with you, tall and ugly, dressed in red, with orange hair and a long scar down the left side of his face."

I didn't say anything. I couldn't. I looked down at the floor and squeezed my hands together.

"Another funny thing," he said. "The nurse who discovered me awake swore there were two people in the room, a man and a boy. The doctors think it was her mind playing tricks and have said it doesn't matter. Strange, though, isn't it?"

"Very strange," I agreed, unable to look him in the eye.

I began noticing changes in myself over the next couple of days. I found it hard getting to sleep when I went to bed, and kept waking in the middle of the night. My hearing improved and I was able to hear people talking from far away. In school, I could listen to voices from the next two rooms, almost as if there were no walls between my class and theirs.

I began to get fitter. I was able to run about the yard during break and lunch without working up a sweat. Nobody could keep up with me. I was also more aware of my body and was able to control it. I could make a football do pretty much what I wanted, dribbling around opponents at will. I scored sixteen goals on Thursday.

I grew stronger, too. I was able to do push-ups and pull-ups now, as many as I liked. I didn't have new muscles — none that I could see — but there was a strength flowing through me which hadn't been there before. I had yet to test it properly but I believed it might be immense.

I tried hiding my new talents but it was difficult. I explained away the running and soccer skills by saying I was exercising and practising a lot more, but other things were trickier.

Like when the bell rang on Thursday at the end of lunch. The ball had just been kicked into the air by the goalie who I'd put sixteen goals past. It was coming towards me, so I stuck up my right hand to catch it. I did, but as I squeezed, my nails sunk in and burst it!

And when I was eating dinner at home that night, I wasn't concentrating. I could hear our next-door neighbours having a fight and I was listening to their argument. I was eating chips and sausages, and after a while I noticed the food was tougher than it should be. I glanced down and realised I'd bitten the head off the fork and was chewing it to pieces! Luckily, no one saw, and I was able to slip it into the dustbin as I was washing up.

Steve rang that Thursday night. He'd been let out of hospital. He was supposed to take things easy for a few days and not come in to school until after the weekend, but he said he was going crazy with boredom and had persuaded his mum to let him come tomorrow.

"You mean you *want* to come to school?" I asked, shocked.

"Sounds weird, doesn't it?" he laughed. "Normally I'm looking for an excuse to stay home. Yet now, when I have one, I want to go! But you don't know how dull it is being stuck indoors alone all the time. It was fun for a couple of days, but a whole week of it... Brrr!"

I thought of telling Steve the truth but wasn't sure how he'd take it. He had *wanted* to become a vampire. I didn't think he'd like knowing Mr Crepsley had picked me instead of him.

And telling Annie was out of the question. She hadn't mentioned Madam Octa since Steve recovered but I often found her watching me. I don't know what was going through her head, but my guess is it was something like: "Steve got better, but it wasn't because of *you*. You had the chance to save him and you didn't. You told a lie and risked his life, just so you wouldn't get into trouble. Would you have done the same if it had been *me*?"

Steve was the centre of attention that Friday. The whole class crowded round and begged for his story. They wanted to know what had poisoned him, how he'd survived, what the hospital had been like, if they'd operated on him, if he had any scars, and so on.

"I don't know what bit me," he said. "I was at Darren's house. I was sitting by the window. I heard a noise but before I could look to see what it was, I got bitten and passed out." This was the story we had agreed upon when I went to visit him at the hospital.

I felt stranger than ever that Friday. I spent the morning gazing round the classroom, feeling out of place. It seemed so pointless. "I shouldn't be here," I kept thinking. "I'm not a normal kid any more. I should be out earning my living as a vampire's assistant. What good will English, history and geography do me now? This isn't my scene."

Tommy and Alan told Steve about my skill on the football field. "He's running like the wind these days," Alan said.

"And playing like Pele," Tommy added.

"Really?" Steve asked, looking at me oddly. "What's brought on the big change, Darren?"

"There isn't any change," I lied. "I'm just on a roll. I'm lucky."

"Listen to Mr Modest!" Tommy laughed. "Mr Dalton has said he might put him forward for the under-seventeen football team. Imagine one of us playing for the under-seventeens! Nobody our age has ever made that team."

"No," Steve mused. "They haven't."

"Aw, it's just Sir talking," I said, trying to brush it aside.

"Maybe," Steve said. "*Maybe.*"

I played badly that lunch-time, on purpose. I could tell Steve was suspicious. I don't think he knew what was going on, but he sensed something was different about me. I ran slowly and missed chances I normally would have put away even without the special powers.

My ploy worked. By the end of the game he'd stopped studying my every move and was beginning to joke with me again. But then something happened which ruined everything.

Alan and me were running for the same ball. He shouldn't have been going for it, because I was closest. But Alan was a bit younger than the rest of us and sometimes acted stupidly. I thought about pulling back but I was sick of playing badly. Lunch was nearly over and I wanted to score at least one goal.

So I decided, the hell with Alan Morris. That's my ball and if he gets in my way, tough!

We clashed with each other just before reaching the ball. Alan gave a yell and went flying. I laughed, trapped the ball under my foot and turned towards goal.

The sight of blood stopped me in my tracks.

Alan had landed awkwardly and cut his left knee. It was a bad gash and blood was welling up. He had started to cry and was making no move to cover it with a tissue or scrap of cloth.

Somebody kicked the ball away from beneath my foot and set off with it. I took no notice. My eyes were focused on Alan. More specifically, on Alan's knee. More specifically still, on Alan's *blood*.

I took a step towards him. Then another. I was standing over him now, blocking the light. He gazed up and must have seen something odd in my face, because he stopped crying and stared at me uneasily.

I dropped to my knees and, before I knew what I was doing, I had covered the cut on his leg with my mouth and was sucking out his blood and gulping it down!

This went on for a few seconds. My eyes were closed and the blood filled my mouth. It tasted lovely. I'm not sure how much I would have drunk or how much harm I would have done to Alan. Luckily, I didn't get the chance to find out.

I became aware of people around me and opened my eyes. Nearly everyone had stopped playing and was staring at me in horror. I removed my lips from Alan's knee and looked around at my friends, wondering how to explain this.

Then the solution hit me and I jumped up and spread my arms. "I am the vampire lord!" I yelled. "I am the king of the undead! I will suck the blood from all of you!"

They stared at me in shock, then laughed. They thought it

was a joke! They thought I was only pretending to be a vampire.

"You're a nutter, Shan," somebody said.

"That's gross!" a girl squealed as fresh blood dripped down my chin. "You should be locked away!"

The bell rang and it was time to return to class. I was feeling pleased with myself. I thought I'd fooled everybody. But then I noticed someone near the back of the crowd and my joy faded. It was Steve, and his dark face told me he knew exactly what had happened. He hadn't been fooled at all.

He *knew*.

CHAPTER TWENTY-EIGHT

I AVOIDED Steve that evening and rushed straight home. I was confused. Why had I attacked Alan? I didn't want to drink anybody's blood. I hadn't been looking for a victim. So how come I'd jumped on him like a wild animal? And what if it happened again? And what if next time there was nobody around to stop me and I went on sucking until...

No, that was a crazy thought. The sight of blood had taken me by surprise, that was all. I hadn't been expecting it. I would learn from this experience and next time I'd be able to hold myself back.

The taste of blood was still in my mouth, so I went to the bathroom and washed it out with several glasses of water, then brushed my teeth.

I studied myself in the mirror. My face looked the same as ever. My teeth weren't any longer or sharper. My eyes and ears were the same. I had the same old body. No extra muscles, no added height, no fresh patches of hair. The only visible difference was in my nails, which had hardened and darkened.

So why was I acting so strangely?

I drew one of my nails along the glass of the mirror and

it made a long deep scratch. "I'll have to be careful of those," I thought to myself.

My attack on Alan aside, I didn't appear to be too badly off. In fact, the more I thought about it, the less dreadful it seemed. OK, it would take a long time to grow up, and I'd have to be careful if I saw fresh blood. Those were downers.

But apart from that, life should be fine. I was stronger than anybody else my age, faster and fitter. I could become an athlete or a boxer or a footballer. My age would work against me but if I was talented enough, that wouldn't matter.

Imagine: a vampire footballer! I'd make millions. I'd be on TV chat shows, people would write books about me, a film would be made of my life, and I might be asked to make a song with a famous band. Maybe I could get work in the movie business as a stuntman for other kids. Or...

My thoughts were interrupted by a knock on the door. "Who is it?" I asked.

"Annie," came the reply. "Are you finished yet? I've been waiting for ages to use the bath."

"Come in," I told her. "I'm done."

She entered. "Admiring yourself in the mirror again?" she asked.

"Of course," I grinned. "Why shouldn't I?"

"If I had a face like yours, I'd stay away from mirrors," she giggled. She had a towel wrapped around her. She turned on the bath taps and ran a hand under the water to make sure it wasn't too hot. Then she sat on the edge of the tub and studied me.

"You look strange," she said.

"I don't," I said. Then, looking in the mirror, I asked: "Do I?"

"Yeah," she said. "I don't know what it is, but there's something different about you."

"You're just imagining things," I told her. "I'm the same as I always was."

"No," she said, shaking her head. "You're definitely… " The tub began filling up, so she stopped speaking and turned aside to turn off the taps. As she was bending over, my eyes focused on the curve of her neck, and suddenly my mouth went dry.

"As I was saying, you look— " she began, turning back around.

She stopped when she saw my eyes.

"Darren?" she asked nervously. "Darren, what are— "

I raised my right hand and she went quiet. Her eyes widened and she stared silently at my fingers as I waved them slowly from side to side, then around in small circles. I wasn't sure how I was doing it, but I was hypnotising her!

"Come here," I growled, voice deeper than normal. Annie rose and obeyed. She moved as if sleepwalking, eyes blank, arms and legs stiff.

When she stopped before me, I traced the outline of her neck with my fingers. I was breathing heavily and seeing her as though through a misty cloud. My tongue slowly licked around my lips and my belly rumbled. The bathroom felt as hot as a furnace, and I could see beads of sweat rolling down Annie's face.

I walked around the back of her, my hands never leaving her flesh. I could feel the veins throbbing as I stroked them, and when I pressed down on one near the bottom of her neck, I could see it standing out, blue and beautiful, begging to be ripped open and sucked dry.

I bared my teeth and leaned forward, jaws wide open.

At the last moment, as my lips touched her neck, I caught sight of my reflection in the mirror, and thankfully that was enough to make me pause.

The face in the mirror was a twisted, unfamiliar mask, full of red eyes, sharp wrinkles and a vicious grin. I lifted my head for a closer look. It was me but at the same time it wasn't. It was like there were two people sharing one body, a normal human boy and a savage animal of the night.

As I stared, the ugly face faded and the urge to drink blood passed. I gazed at Annie, horrified. I'd been about to *bite* her! I would have *fed* on my own sister!

I fell away from her with a cry and covered my face with my hands, afraid of the mirror and what I might see. Annie staggered backwards, then looked around the bathroom in a dazed kind of way.

"What's going on?" she asked. "I feel odd. I came in for a bath, didn't I? Is it ready?"

"Yes," I said softly. "It's ready."

I was ready too. Ready to become a vampire!

"I'll leave you to get on with it," I said, and let myself out.

I fell against the wall in the hall, where I spent a couple of minutes taking deep breaths and trying to calm down.

It couldn't be controlled. The thirst for blood was something I wouldn't be able to beat. I didn't even have to see spilt blood now. Just thinking of it had been enough to bring out the monster in me.

I stumbled to my room and collapsed upon my bed. I cried as I lay there, because I knew my life as a human had come to an end. I could no longer live as plain old Darren Shan. The vampire in me could not be controlled. Sooner or later it would make me do something terrible and I would end up killing Mum or Dad or Annie.

I couldn't let that happen. I *wouldn't*. My life was no longer important, but those of my friends and family were. For their sakes, I would have to travel far away, to a place where I could do no harm.

I waited for dark to fall, then let myself out. No hanging around this time until my parents fell asleep. I didn't dare, because I knew one of them would come to my room before going to bed. I could picture it, Mum bending over to kiss me goodnight, getting the shock of her life as I bit into her neck.

I didn't leave a note or take anything with me. I wasn't able to think about such things. All I knew was, I had to get out, the sooner the better. Anything that delayed my exit was bad.

I walked quickly and was soon at the theatre. It no longer looked scary. I was used to it. Besides, vampires have nothing to fear from dark, haunted buildings.

Mr Crepsley was waiting for me inside the front door.

"I heard you coming," he said. "You lasted longer in the world of humans than I thought."

"I sucked blood from one of my best friends," I told him. "And I almost bit my younger sister."

"You escaped lightly," he said. "Many vampires kill someone close to them before realising they are doomed."

"There's no way back, is there?" I asked sadly. "No magic potion to make me human again or keep me from attacking people?"

"The only thing that can stop you now," he said, "is the good old stake through the heart."

"Very well," I sighed. "I don't like it, but I guess I've no other choice. I'm yours. I won't run away again. Do with me as you wish."

He nodded slowly. "You probably will not believe this," he said, "but I know what you are going through and I feel sorry for you." He shook his head. "But that is neither here nor there. We have work to do and cannot afford to waste time. Come, Darren Shan," he said, taking my hand. "We have much to do before you can assume your rightful place as my assistant."

"Like what?" I asked, confused.

"First of all," he said, with a sly smile, "we have to *kill you!*"

CHAPTER TWENTY-NINE

I SPENT my last weekend saying silent goodbyes. I visited every one of my favourite spots: library, swimming pool, cinema, parks, football stadium. I went to some of the places with Mum or Dad, some with Alan Morris or Tommy Jones. I would have liked to spend time with Steve but couldn't bear to face him.

I got the feeling, every so often, that I was being followed, and the hairs on the back of my neck stood on end. But whenever I turned to look, nobody was there. Eventually I put it down to nerves and ignored it.

I treated every minute with my family and friends as if it was special. I paid close attention to their faces and voices, so I would never forget. I knew I'd never see these people again and that tore me apart inside, but it was the way it had to be. There was no going back.

They could do nothing wrong that weekend. Mum's kisses didn't embarrass me, Dad's orders didn't bother me, Alan's stupid jokes didn't annoy me.

I spent more time with Annie than with anybody else. I was going to miss her the most. I gave her piggyback rides and swung her round by the arms and took her to the football stadium with me and Tommy. I even played with her dolls!

Sometimes I felt like crying. I'd look at Mum or Dad or Annie and realise how much I loved them, how empty my life would be without them. I had to turn aside at moments like that and take long, deep breaths. A couple of times that didn't work and I rushed away to cry in private.

I think they guessed something was wrong. Mum came into my room that Saturday night and stayed for ages, tucking me into bed, telling me stories, listening to me talk. It had been years since we'd spent time together like that. I felt sorry, after she'd gone, that we hadn't had more nights like this.

In the morning, Dad asked if there was anything I wanted to discuss with him. He said I was a growing lad and would be going through lots of changes, and he'd understand if I had mood swings or wanted to go off by myself. But he would always be there for me to talk to.

"*You'll* be there, but *I* won't be!" I felt like crying, but I kept quiet, nodded my head and thanked him.

I behaved as perfectly as possible. I wanted to leave a fine final impression, so they would remember me as a good son, a good brother, a good friend. I didn't want anybody thinking badly of me when I was gone.

Dad was going to take us out to a restaurant for dinner that Sunday, but I asked if we could stay home to eat. This would be my last meal with them and I wanted it to be special. When I was looking back on it in later years, I wanted to be able to remember us together, at home, a happy family.

Mum cooked my favourite food: chicken, roast potatoes, corn-on-the-cob. Annie and me had freshly squeezed orange juice to drink. Mum and Dad shared a bottle of wine. We had strawberry cheesecake for dessert. Everybody was in good form. We sang songs. Dad cracked terrible jokes. Mum played a tune with a pair of spoons. Annie recited a few poems. Everybody joined in for a game of charades.

It was a day I wished would never end. But, of course, all days must, and finally, as it always does, the sun dropped and the darkness of night crept across the sky.

Dad looked up after a while, then at his watch. "Time for bed," he said. "You two have school in the morning."

"No," I thought, "I don't. I don't have school ever again." That should have cheered me up — but all I could think was: "No school means no Mr Dalton, no friends, no football, no school trips."

I delayed going to bed as long as I could. I spent ages taking off my clothes and putting on my pyjamas; longer still washing my hands and face and teeth. Then, when it could be avoided no longer, I went downstairs to the living room, where Mum and Dad were talking. They looked up, surprised to see me.

"Are you all right, Darren?" Mum asked.

"I'm fine," I said.

"You're not feeling sick?"

"I'm fine," I assured her. "I just wanted to say goodnight." I put my arms around Dad, then kissed him on the cheek. Next I did the same with Mum. "Goodnight," I said to each.

"This is one for the books," Dad laughed, rubbing his cheek where I had kissed him. "How long since he kissed the two of us goodnight, Angie?"

"Too long," Mum smiled, patting my head.

"I love you," I told them. "I know I haven't said it very often, but I do. I love the both of you and always will."

"We love you too," Mum said. "Don't we, Dermot?"

"Of course we do," Dad said.

"Well, *tell* him," she insisted.

Dad sighed. "I love you, Darren," he said, rolling his eyes in

163

a way he knew would make me laugh. Then he gave me a hug. "Really I do," he said, serious this time.

I left them then. I stood outside the door a while, listening to them talk, reluctant to depart.

"What do you think brought that on?" Mum asked.

"Kids," Dad snorted. "Who knows how their minds work?"

"There's something up," Mum said. "He's been acting oddly for some time now."

"Maybe he's got a girlfriend," Dad suggested.

"Maybe," Mum said, but didn't sound convinced.

I'd lingered long enough. I was afraid, if I waited any longer, I might rush into the room and tell them what was really the matter. If I did, they'd stop me from going ahead with Mr Crepsley's plan. They'd say that vampires weren't real and fight to keep me with them, in spite of the danger.

I thought of Annie and how close I'd come to biting her, and knew I must not let them stop me.

I trudged upstairs to my room. It was a warm night and the window was open. That was important.

Mr Crepsley was waiting in the wardrobe. He emerged when he heard me closing the door. "It is stuffy in there," he complained. "I feel sorry for Madam Octa, having had to spend so much time in— "

"Shut up," I told him.

"No need to be rude," he sniffed. "I was merely passing a comment."

"Well, don't," I said. "You might not think much of this place but I do. This has been my home, my room, my wardrobe, ever since I can remember. And I'm never going to see it again after tonight. This is my last little while here. So don't badmouth it, all right?"

"I am sorry," he said.

I took one long last look around the room, then sighed unhappily. I pulled a bag out from underneath the bed and handed it to Mr Crepsley. "What is this?" he asked suspiciously.

"Some personal stuff," I told him. "My diary. A picture of my family. A couple of other bits and pieces. Nothing that will be missed. Will you mind it for me?"

"Yes," he said.

"But only if you promise not to look through it," I said.

"Vampires have no secrets from each other," he said. But, when he saw my face, he tutted lightly and shrugged. "I will not open it," he promised.

"All right," I said, taking a deep breath. "Do you have the potion?" He nodded and handed over a small dark bottle. I looked inside. The liquid was dark and thick and foul-smelling.

Mr Crepsley moved behind me and laid his hands on my neck.

"You're sure this will work?" I asked nervously.

"Trust me," he said.

"I always thought a broken neck meant people couldn't walk or move," I said.

"No," he replied. "The bones of the neck do not matter. Paralysis only happens if the spinal cord – a long muscle running down the middle of the neck – breaks. I will be careful not to damage it."

"Won't the doctors think it's odd?" I asked.

"They will not check," he said. "The potion will slow your heart down so much, they will be sure you are dead. They will find the broken neck and put two and two together. If you were older, they might go ahead with an autopsy. But no doctor likes cutting a child open.

"Now, are you totally clear on what is going to happen and how you must act?" he asked.

"Yes," I said.

"There must be no mistakes," he warned. "If you make just one slip our plans will fall apart."

"I'm not a fool! I know what to do!" I snapped.

"Then do it," he said.

So I did.

With one angry gesture, I swallowed the contents of the bottle. I grimaced at the taste, then shuddered as my body started to stiffen. There wasn't much pain but an icy feeling spread through my bones and veins. My teeth began to chatter.

It took about ten minutes for the poison to work its deadly charms. At the end of that time I couldn't move any of my limbs, my lungs weren't working (well, they were, but very, very slowly) and my heart had stopped (again, not fully, but enough for its beat to be undetectable).

"I am going to snap the neck now," Mr Crepsley said, and I heard a quick clicking sound as he jerked my head to one side. I couldn't feel anything: my senses were dead. "There," he said. "That should do it. Now I am going to toss you out of the window."

He carried me over and stood there a moment with me, breathing in the night air.

"I have to toss you hard enough to make it look genuine," he said. "You might break some bones in the fall. They will start hurting when the potion wears off after a few days but I will fix them up later on.

"Here we go!"

He picked me up, paused a moment, then hurled me out and down.

I fell quickly, the house whizzing past in a blur, and landed heavily on my back. My eyes were open and I found myself staring at a drain at the foot of the house.

For a while my body went undetected, so I lay there, listening to the sounds of the night. In the end, a passing neighbour spotted me and investigated. I couldn't see his face but I heard his gasp when he turned me over and saw my lifeless body.

He rushed straight around to the front of the house and pounded on the door. I could hear his voice as he shouted for my mother and father. Then their voices as he led them round back. They thought he was pulling their leg or had been mistaken. My father was marching angrily and muttering to himself.

The footsteps stopped when they rounded the bend and saw me. For a long, terrible moment there was complete silence. Then Dad and Mum rushed forward and picked me up.

"Darren!" Mum screamed, clutching me to her chest.

"Let go, Angie," Dad shouted, prying me free and laying me down on the grass.

"What's wrong with him, Dermot?" Mum wailed.

"I don't know. He must have fallen." Dad stood and gazed up at my open bedroom window. I could see his hands flexing into fists.

"He's not moving," Mum said calmly, then grabbed me and shook me fiercely. "He's not moving!" she screamed. "He's not moving. He's— "

Dad once again eased her hands away. He beckoned our neighbour over and handed Mum to him. "Take her inside," he said softly. "Ring for an ambulance. I'll stay here and look after Darren."

"Is he... dead?" our neighbour asked. Mum moaned loudly when he said it and buried her face in her hands.

Dad shook his head softly. "No," he said, giving Mum's shoulder a light squeeze. "He's just paralysed, like his friend was."

Mum lowered her hands. "Like Steve?" she asked half-hopefully.

"Yes," Dad smiled. "And he'll snap out of it like Steve. Now go ring for help, OK?"

Mum nodded, then hurried away with our neighbour. Dad held his smile until she was out of sight, then bent over me, checked my eyes and felt my wrist for a pulse. When he found no sign of life, he laid me back down, brushed a lock of hair out of my eyes, then did something I'd never expected to see.

He started to cry.

And that was how I came to enter a new, miserable phase of my life, namely – *death*.

CHAPTER THIRTY

IT DIDN'T take the doctors long to pronounce their verdict. They couldn't find any breath or pulse or movement. It was an open-and-shut case as far as they were concerned.

The worst thing was knowing what was going on around me. I wished that I'd asked Mr Crepsley to give me another potion, which could have put me to sleep. It was terrible, hearing Mum and Dad crying, Annie screaming for me to come back.

Friends of the family began arriving after a couple of hours, the cue for more sobbing and moans.

I'd have loved to avoid this. I would have rather run away with Mr Crepsley in the middle of the night, but he'd told me that wasn't possible.

"If you run away," he'd said, "they would follow. There would be posters up everywhere, pictures in the papers and with the police. We would know no peace."

Faking my death was the only way. If they thought I was dead, I'd be free. Nobody comes searching for a dead person.

Now, as I heard the sadness, I cursed both Mr Crepsley and myself. I shouldn't have done it. I shouldn't have put them through this.

Still, looking on the bright side, at least this would be the end of it. They were sad, and would be for some time, but they would get over it eventually (I hoped). If I'd run away, the misery could have lasted forever: they might have lived the rest of their lives hoping I'd come back, searching, believing I would one day return.

The undertaker arrived and cleared the room of visitors. He and a nurse undressed me and examined my body. Some of my senses were returning and I could feel his cold hands prodding and poking me.

"He's in excellent condition," he said softly to the nurse. "Firm, fresh and unmarked. I'll have very little to do with this one. Just some rouge to make him look a little redder round the cheeks."

He rolled up my eyelids. He was a chubby, happy-looking man. I was afraid he'd spot life in my eyes but he didn't. All he did was roll my head gently from side to side, which made the broken bones in my neck creak.

"So fragile a creature is man," he sighed, then went ahead with the rest of the examination.

They took me back home that night and laid me in the living room on a long table with a large cloth spread across it, so people could come and say goodbye.

It was weird, hearing all those people discussing me as though I wasn't there, talking about my life and what I'd been like as a baby and how fine a boy I was and what a good man I would have grown up to be if I'd lived.

What a shock they'd have got if I leaped up and shouted: "*Boo!*"

Time dragged. I don't think I can explain how boring it was to lie still for hours on end, unable to move or laugh or scratch my nose. I couldn't even stare at the ceiling because my eyes were shut!

I had to be careful as feelings returned to my body. Mr Crepsley had told me this would happen, that tingles and itches would start, long before I fully recovered. I couldn't move, but if I'd made a real effort, I could have twitched a little, which might have given the game away.

The itches nearly drove me mad. I tried ignoring them but it was impossible. They were everywhere, scampering up and down my body like tiny spiders. They were worst around my head and neck, where the bones had snapped.

People finally began leaving. It must have been late, because soon the room was empty and totally silent. I lay there by myself for a time, enjoying the quiet.

And then I heard a noise.

The door to the room was opening, very slowly and very quietly.

Footsteps crossed the room and stopped by the table. My insides went cold, and it wasn't because of the potion. Who was here? For a moment I thought it might be Mr Crepsley but he had no reason to come creeping into the house. We were set to meet at a later date.

Whoever it was, he – or she – was keeping very quiet. For a couple of minutes there was no sound at all.

Then I felt hands on my face.

He raised my eyelids and shone a small torch onto my pupils. The room was too dark for me to see who he was. He grunted, lowered the lids, then pried open my mouth and laid something on my tongue: it felt like a piece of thin paper but it had a strange, bitter taste.

After removing the object from my mouth, he picked up my hands and examined the fingertips. Next there was the sound of a camera taking photos.

Finally he stuck a sharp object – it felt like a needle – into me. He was careful not to prick me in places where I would bleed, and stayed away from my vital organs. My senses had partially returned, but not fully, so the needle didn't cause much pain.

After that, he left. I heard his footsteps crossing the room, as quietly as before, then the door opening and closing, and that was that. The visitor, whoever it had been, was gone, leaving me puzzled and a little bit scared.

Early the next morning, Dad came in and sat with me. He spoke for a long time, telling me all the things he'd had planned for me, the college I would have gone to, the job he'd wanted for me. He cried a lot.

Towards the end, Mum came in and sat with him. They cried on each other's shoulders and tried to comfort themselves. They said they still had Annie and could maybe have another child or adopt one. At least it had been quick and I hadn't been in pain. And they would always have their memories.

I hated being the cause of so much hurt. I would have given anything in the world to spare them this.

There was a lot of activity later that day. A coffin was brought in and I was laid inside. A priest came and sat with the family and their friends. People streamed in and out of the room.

I heard Annie crying, begging me to stop fooling and sit up. It would have been much easier if they'd taken her away, but I guess they didn't want her to grow up feeling they'd robbed her of her chance to say goodbye to her brother.

Finally, the lid was placed on the coffin and screwed into place. I was lifted off the table and led out to the hearse. We drove slowly to church, where I couldn't hear much of what was being said. Then, with Mass out of the way, they carried me to the graveyard, where I could hear every word of the priest's speech and the sobs and moans of the mourners.

And then they buried me.

CHAPTER THIRTY-ONE

ALL SOUNDS faded away as they lowered me down the dark, dank hole. There was a jolt when the coffin hit bottom, then the rain-like sound of the first handfuls of soil being tossed upon the lid.

There was a long silence after that, until the grave diggers began shovelling the earth back into the grave.

The first few clods fell like bricks. The heavy dull thuds shook the coffin. As the grave filled and earth piled up between me and the topside world, the sounds of the living grew softer, until finally they were only faraway muffles.

At the end there were faint pounding noises, as they patted the mound of earth flat.

And then complete silence.

I lay in the quiet darkness, listening to the earth settle, imagining the sound of worms crawling towards me through the dirt. I'd thought it would be scary but it was actually quite peaceful. I felt safe down here, protected from the world.

I spent the time thinking about the last few weeks, the flyer for the freak show, the strange force that had made me close my eyes and reach blindly for the ticket, my first glimpse of the dark theatre, the cool balcony where I had watched Steve talking with Mr Crepsley.

There were so many vital moments. If I'd missed the ticket, I wouldn't be here. If I hadn't gone to the show, I wouldn't be here. If I hadn't stuck around to see what Steve was up to, I wouldn't be here. If I hadn't stolen Madam Octa, I wouldn't be here. If I'd said no to Mr Crepsley's offer, I wouldn't be here.

A world of "ifs", but it made no difference. What was done was done. If I could go back in time...

But I couldn't. The past was behind me. The best thing now would be to stop looking over my shoulder. It was time to forget the past and look to the present and future.

As the hours passed, movement returned. It came to my fingers first, which curled into fists, then slipped from my chest, where they had been crossed by the undertaker. I flexed them several times, slowly, working the itches out of my palms.

My eyes opened next but that wasn't much good. Open or closed, it was all the same down here: perfect darkness.

The feelings brought pain. My back ached from where I'd fallen out of the window. My lungs, and heart – having been out of the habit of beating – hurt. My legs were cramped, my neck was stiff. The only part of me which escaped the pain was my big right toe!

It was when I started breathing that I began to worry about the air in the coffin. Mr Crepsley had said I could survive for up to a week in my coma-like state. I didn't need to eat or use the toilet or breathe. But now that my breath was back, I became aware of the small amount of air and how quickly I was using it up.

I didn't panic. Panic would make me gasp and use more air. I remained calm and breathed softly. Lay as still as I could: movement makes you breathe more.

I had no way of knowing the time. I tried counting inside my head but kept losing track of the numbers and having to go back and start over.

I sang silent songs to myself and told stories beneath my

breath. I wished they'd buried me with a TV or a radio, but I guess there's not much call for such items among the dead.

Finally, after what seemed like several centuries stacked one on top of the other, the sounds of digging reached my ears.

He dug quicker than any human, so fast it seemed he wasn't digging at all, but rather sucking the soil out. He reached me in what must have been record time, less than a quarter of an hour. As far as I was concerned, it wasn't a moment too soon.

He knocked three times on the coffin lid, then started unscrewing it. It took a couple of minutes, then he threw the lid wide open and I found myself staring up at the most beautiful night sky I had ever seen.

I took a deep breath and sat up, coughing. It was a fairly dark night but after spending so much time underground it seemed bright as day to me.

"Are you all right?" Mr Crepsley asked.

"I feel dead tired," I grinned weakly.

He smiled at the joke. "Stand up so I can examine you," he said. I winced as I stood: I had pins and needles all over. He ran his fingers lightly up my back, then over my front. "You were lucky," he said. "No broken bones. Just a bit of bruising which will die down after a couple of days."

He pulled himself up out of the grave, then reached down and gave me a hand up. I was still pretty stiff and sore.

"I feel like a pincushion that's been squashed," I complained.

"It will take a few days for the after-effects to pass," he said. "But do not worry: you are in good shape. We are lucky they buried you today. If they had waited another day to put you under, you would be feeling much worse."

He hopped back into the grave and closed the coffin lid. When he emerged, he picked up his shovel and began tossing the earth back in.

"Do you want me to help?" I asked.

"No," he said. "You would slow me down. Go for a stroll and walk some of the stiffness out of your bones. I will call when I am ready to move on."

"Did you bring my bag?" I asked.

He nodded at a nearby headstone, from which the bag was hanging.

I got the bag and checked to see if he'd searched it. There was no sign of his having invaded my privacy, but I couldn't tell for sure. I'd just have to take him at his word. Anyway, it didn't matter much: there was nothing in my diary he didn't already know.

I went for a walk among the graves, testing my limbs, shaking my legs and arms, enjoying it. Any feeling, even pins and needles, was better than none at all.

My eyes were stronger than ever before. I was able to read names and dates on headstones from several metres away. It was the vampire blood in me. After all, didn't vampires spend their whole lives in the dark? I knew I was only a half-vampire, but all the—

Suddenly, as I was thinking about my new powers, a hand reached out from behind one of the graves, wrapped itself around my mouth, then dragged me down to the ground and out of sight of Mr Crepsley!

I shook my head and opened my mouth to scream, but then saw something that stopped me dead in my tracks. My attacker, whoever he was, had a hammer and a large wooden stake, the tip of which was pointing *directly at my heart!*

CHAPTER THIRTY-TWO

"IF YOU move even a fraction," my attacker warned, "I'll drive this right through you without blinking!"

The chilling words didn't have half as much impact on me as the familiar voice which uttered them.

"Steve?!?" I gasped, glancing up from the tip of the stake to find his face. It was him, sure enough, trying to look brave, but really quite terrified. "Steve, what the— " I began but he cut me short with a poke of the stake.

"Not a word!" he hissed, crouching down behind the stone pillar. "I don't want your friend overhearing."

"My...? Oh, you mean Mr Crepsley," I said.

"Larten Crepsley, Vur Horston," Steve sneered. "I don't care what you call him. He's a vampire. That's all that bothers me."

"What are you doing here?" I whispered.

"Vampire hunting," he growled, prodding me again with the stake. "And lookee here: seems like I found me a pair!"

"Listen," I said, more annoyed than worried (if he was going to kill me, he would have done it immediately, not sit around talking first, like they do in the movies), "if you're going to stick that thing in me, do it. If you want to talk, put it away. I'm sore enough as it is without you making new holes in me."

He stared, then pulled the stake back a few centimetres.

"Why are you here?" I asked. "How did you know to come?"

"I was following you," he said. "I followed you all weekend after seeing what you did to Alan. I saw Crepsley going into your house. I saw him toss you out the window."

"You're the one who sneaked into the living room!" I gasped, remembering the mysterious late-night visitor.

"Yes," he nodded. "The doctors were very quick to sign your death certificate. I wanted to check for myself, to see if you were still ticking."

"The piece of paper in my mouth?" I asked.

"Litmus paper," he said. "It changes colour when you stick it on a damp surface. When you stick it on a *living* body. That and the marks on the fingers tipped me off."

"You know about the marks on the fingers?" I asked, amazed.

"I read about it in a very old book," he said. "The same one, in fact, that I found Vur Horston's portrait in. There was no mention of it anywhere else, so I thought it was just another vampire myth. But then I studied your fingers and— "

He stopped and cocked his head. I realised I could no longer hear digging sounds. For a moment there was silence. Then Mr Crepsley's voice hissed across the graveyard.

"Darren, where are you?" he called. "Darren?"

Steve's face collapsed with fear. I could hear his heart beating and see the beads of sweat rolling down his cheeks. He didn't know what to do. He hadn't thought this through.

"I'm fine," I shouted, causing Steve to jump.

"Where are you?" Mr Crepsley asked.

"Over here," I replied, standing, ignoring Steve's stake. "My legs were weak, so I lay down for a minute."

"Are you all right?" he asked.

"I'm fine," I said. "I'll rest a bit more, then try them again. Give me a shout when you're ready."

I squatted back down so I was face to face with Steve. He didn't look so brave any longer. The tip of the stake was pointing down at the ground, a threat no more, and his whole body sagged miserably. I felt sorry for him.

"Why did you come here, Steve?" I asked.

"To kill you," he said.

"To *kill* me? For heaven's sake, why?" I asked.

"You're a vampire," he said. "What other reason do I need?"

"But you've nothing against vampires," I reminded him. "*You* wanted to become one."

"Yes," he snarled. "*I* wanted to, but *you're* the one who did. You planned this all along, didn't you? You told him I was evil. You made him reject me so that you could— "

"You're talking nonsense," I sighed. "I never wanted to become a vampire. I only agreed to join him in order to save your life. You would have died if I hadn't become his assistant."

"A likely story," he snorted. "To think I used to believe you were my friend. Hah!"

"I am your friend!" I cried. "Steve, you don't understand. I would never do anything to harm you. I hate what's happened to me. I only did it to— "

"Spare me the sob story," he sniffed. "How long were you planning this? You must have gone to him that night of the freak show. That's how you got Madam Octa, wasn't it? He gave her to you in return for your becoming his assistant."

"No, Steve, that's not true. You mustn't believe that." But he did believe it. I could see it in his eyes. Nothing I said was going to change his opinion. As far as he was concerned, I'd betrayed him. I had stolen the life he felt should have been his. He would never forgive me.

"I'm going now," he said, starting to crawl away. "I thought I'd be able to kill you tonight, but I was wrong. I'm too young. I'm not strong enough or brave enough.

"But heed this, Darren Shan," he said. "I'll grow. I'll get older and stronger and braver. I'm going to devote my entire life to developing my body and my mind, and when the day comes... when I'm ready... when I'm fully equipped and properly prepared...

"*I'm going to hunt you down and kill you,*" he vowed. "I'm going to become the world's best vampire hunter and there won't be a single hole you can find that I won't be able to find too. Not a hole nor a rock nor a cellar.

"I'll track you to the ends of the Earth if I have to," he said, face glowing madly. "You and your mentor. And when I find you, I'll drive steel-tipped stakes through your hearts, then chop off your heads and fill them with garlic. Then I'll burn you to ashes and scatter you across running water. I won't take any chances. I'll make sure you never come back from the grave again!"

He paused, produced a knife, and cut a small cross into the flesh of his left palm. He held it up so I could see the blood dripping from the wound.

"On this blood, I so swear it!" he declared, then turned and ran, disappearing in seconds into the shadows of the night.

I could have run after him, following the trail of blood. If I'd called Mr Crepsley, we could have tracked him down and put an end to both Steve Leopard and his threats. It would have been the wise thing to do.

But I didn't. I couldn't. He was my friend...

CHAPTER THIRTY-THREE

MR CREPSLEY was smoothing over the mound of earth when I returned. I watched him work. The shovel was large and heavy but he handled it as if it was made out of paper. I wondered how strong he was and how strong I would one day be.

I considered telling him about Steve but was afraid he'd go after him. Steve had suffered enough. Besides, his threat was an idle one. He'd forget about me and Mr Crepsley in a few weeks, when something new grabbed his attention.

I hoped.

Mr Crepsley looked up and frowned. "Are you sure you are all right?" he asked. "You seem very uptight."

"So would you if you'd spent the day in a coffin," I replied.

He laughed out loud. "Master Shan, I have spent more time in coffins than many of the truly dead!" He gave the grave one last hard whack, then broke the shovel into little pieces and tossed them away. "Is the stiffness wearing off?" he asked.

"It's better than it was," I said, twisting my arms and waist. "I wouldn't like to fake my death too often though."

"No," he mused. "Well, hopefully it will not be necessary again. It is a dangerous stunt. Many things can go wrong."

I stared at him. "You told me I'd be safe as houses," I said.

"I lied. The potion sometimes drives its patients too far towards death and they never recover. And I could not be sure they would not perform an autopsy on you. And... Do you want to hear all this?" he asked.

"No," I said sickly. "I don't." I took an angry swing at him. He ducked out of the way easily, laughing as he did.

"You told me it was safe!" I shouted. "You lied!"

"I had to," he said. "There was no other way."

"What if I'd died?" I snapped.

He shrugged. "I would be down one assistant. No great loss. I am sure I could have found another."

"You... you... Oh!" I kicked the ground angrily. There were lots of things I could have called him but I didn't like using bad language in the presence of the dead. I'd tell him what I thought about his trickery later.

"Are you ready to go?" he asked.

"Give me a minute," I said. I jumped up on one of the taller headstones and gazed around at the town. I couldn't see much from here but this would be my last glimpse of the place where I had been born and lived, so I took my time and treated every dark alley as a posh cul-de-sac, every crumbling bungalow as a sheikh's palace, every two-storey building as a skyscraper.

"You will grow used to leaving after a time," Mr Crepsley said. He was standing on the stone behind me, perched on little more than thin air. His face was gloomy. "Vampires are always saying goodbye. We never stop anywhere very long. We are forever picking up our roots and moving on to pastures new. It is our way."

"Is the first time the hardest?" I asked.

"Yes," he said, nodding. "But it never gets easy."

"How long before I get used to it?" I wanted to know.

"Maybe a few decades," he said. "Maybe longer."

Decades. He said it as though he was talking of months.

"Can we never make friends?" I asked. "Can we never have homes or wives or families?"

"No," he sighed. "Never."

"Does it get lonely?" I asked.

"Terribly so," he admitted.

I nodded sadly. At least he was being truthful. As I've said before, I'd always rather the truth – however unpleasant it might be – than a lie. You know where you stand with the truth.

"OK," I said, hopping down. "I'm ready." I picked up my bag and dusted some graveyard dirt from it.

"You may ride on my back if you wish," Mr Crepsley offered.

"No, thank you," I replied politely. "Maybe later, but I'd rather walk the stiffness out of my legs first."

"Very well," he said.

I rubbed my belly and listened to it growl. "I haven't eaten since Sunday," I told him. "I'm hungry."

"Me too," he said. Then he took my hand in his and grinned bloodthirstily. "Let us go *eat*."

I took a deep breath and tried not to think about what would be on the menu. I nodded nervously and squeezed his hand. We turned and faced away from the graves. Then, side by side, the vampire and his assistant, we began walking…

…into the night.

TO BE CONTINUED…

FOR A TASTE OF THE NEXT BOOK IN
THE SAGA OF DARREN SHAN,
COME OF AGE AND EXPLORE THE DARKNESS WITH...

THE VAMPIRE'S ASSISTANT

TURN OVER THE PAGE IF YOU DARE TO READ ON...?

It was a dry, warm night, and Stanley Collins had decided to walk home after the Scouts meeting. It wasn't a very long walk — less than a mile — and though the night was dark, he knew every step of the way as surely as he knew how to tie a reef knot.

Stanley was a Scout Master. He loved the Scouts. He'd been one when he was a boy and kept in contact when he grew up. He'd turned his own three sons into first-rate Scouts and, now that they'd grown up and left home, was helping the local kids.

Stanley walked quickly to keep warm, he was only wearing shorts and a T-shirt, and even though it was a nice night, his arms and legs were soon covered in goosebumps. He didn't mind. His wife would have a lovely cup of hot chocolate and currant buns waiting for him when he got home. He'd enjoy them all the more after a good, brisk walk.

Trees grew along both sides of the road home, making it very dark and dangerous for anyone who wasn't used to it. But Stanley had no fears. On the contrary, he loved the night. He enjoyed listening to the sound of his feet crunching through the grass and briars.

Crunch. Crunch. Crunch.

He smiled. When his sons were young, he'd often pretend there were monsters lying in wait up in the trees as they walked home. He'd make scary noises and shake the leaves of low-hanging branches when the boys weren't looking. Sometimes they'd burst into screams and run for home at top speed, and Stanley would follow after them, laughing.

Crunch. Crunch. Crunch.

Sometimes, if he was having trouble getting to sleep at night, he would imagine the sounds of his feet as they made their way home, and that always helped him drift off into a happy dream.

Crunch. Crunch. Crunch.

It was the nicest sound in the world, as far as Stanley was

concerned. It was a great, safe feeling, to know you were all alone and safe as can be.

Crunch. Crunch. Crunch.

Snap.

Stanley stopped and frowned. That had sounded like a stick breaking – but how could it have been? He would have felt it if he'd stepped on a twig. And there were no cows or sheep in the nearby fields.

He stood still for about half a minute, listening curiously. When there were no more sounds, he shook his head and smiled. It had been his imagination playing tricks on him, that was all. He'd tell the wife about it when he got home and they'd have a good old laugh.

He started walking again.

Crunch. Crunch. Crunch.

There. Back to the familiar sounds. There was nobody else about. He would have heard more than a single branch snapping if there was. Nobody could creep up on Stanley J. Collins. He was a trained Scout Master. His ears were as sharp as a fox's.

Crunch. Crunch. Crunch. Crunch. Cru—

Snap.

Stanley stopped again and, for the first time, the fingers of fear began to squeeze around his beating heart.

That hadn't been his imagination. He'd heard it, clear as a bell. A twig snapping, somewhere overhead. And before it snapped – had there been the slightest rustling sound, like something moving?

Stanley gazed up at the trees but it was too dark to see. There could have been a monster the size of a car up there and he wouldn't have been able to spot it. Ten monsters, A hundred! A thou—

Oh, that was silly. There were no monsters in the trees.

Monsters didn't exist. Everyone knew that. Monsters weren't real. It was a squirrel or an owl up there, something ordinary like that.

Stanley raised a foot and began to bring it down.

Snap.

His foot hung in the air, mid-step, and his heart pounded quickly. That was no squirrel! The sound was too sharp. Something *big* was up there. Something that shouldn't be up there. Something that had never been up there before. Something that—

Snap!

The sound was closer this time, lower down, and suddenly Stanley could stand it no longer.

He began to run.

Stanley was a large man, but pretty fit for his age. Still, it had been a long time since he'd run this fast, and after a hundred metres he was out of breath and had a stitch in his side.

He slowed to a halt and bent over, gasping for air.

Crunch.

His head shot up.

Crunch. Crunch. Crunch.

There were footsteps coming towards him! Slow, heavy footsteps. Stanley listened, terrified, as they came closer and closer. Had the monster leapt ahead of him through the trees? Had it climbed down? Was it coming to finish him off? Was it. . .

Crunch. Crunch.

The footsteps stopped and Stanley was able to make out a figure in the darkness. It was smaller than he'd expected, no bigger than a boy. He took a deep breath, straightened up, gathered his courage about him like a cloak, and stepped forward for a better look.

It *was* only a boy! A small, frightened-looking boy, dressed in a dirty suit.

Stanley smiled and shook his head. What a fool he'd been!

The wife would have a field day when he told her about this.

"Are you OK, lad?" Stanley asked him.

The boy didn't answer.

Stanley didn't recognise the youngster, but there were a lot of new families around these days. He no longer knew every child in the neighbourhood.

"Can I help you?" he asked. "Are you lost?"

The boy shook his head slowly. There was something strange about him. Something that suddenly made Stanley feel uneasy. It might have been the effect of the darkness and the shadows. . . but the boy looked very pale, very thin, very. . . *hungry*.

"Are you all right?" Stanley asked again, stepping closer. "Can I—"

Snap!

The sound came from directly overhead, loud and menacing.

The boy leapt back quickly, out of the way.

Stanley just had time to glance upwards and see a huge red shape, which might have been some sort of bat, falling through the branches of the trees, almost faster than his eye could follow.

And then the red thing was on him. Stanley opened his mouth to scream, but before he could, the monster's hands — claws? — clamped over his mouth. There was a brief struggle, then Stanley was sliding onto the ground, unconscious, unseeing, unknowing.

Above him, the two creatures of the night moved in for the feed.

DARREN SHAN

Freak out your friends!

Visit the Scare a Mortal Portal at

WWW.DEMONFREAK.COM

to personalise a video that'll give
your friends the fright of their life!